Seeing Red

Anne Louise MacDonald

KCP Fiction

KCP Fiction is an imprint of Kids Can Press

Kids Can Press acknowledges the financial support of the Government of Ontario, through the Ontario Media Development Corporation's Ontario Book Initiative; the Ontario Arts Council; the Canada Council for the Arts; and the Government of Canada, through the BPIDP, for our publishing activity.

Published in Canada by
Kids Can Press Ltd.
29 Birch Avenue
Toronto, ON M4V 1E2

Published in the U.S. by
Kids Can Press Ltd.
2250 Military Road
Tonawanda, NY 14150

www.kidscanpress.com

Edited by Charis Wahl
Cover designed by Marie Bartholomew
Cover images © 2009 Irene Luxbacher and Jupiterimages Corporation
Interior designed by Julia Naimska

Printed and bound in Canada

The hardcover edition of this book is smyth sewn casebound.
The paperback edition of this book is limp sewn with a drawn-on cover.

CM 09 0 9 8 7 6 5 4 3 2 1
CM PA 09 0 9 8 7 6 5 4 3 2 1

Library and Archives Canada Cataloguing in Publication

MacDonald, Anne Louise, 1955–
    Seeing red / written by Anne MacDonald.

ISBN 978-1-55453-291-9 (bound).   ISBN 978-1-55453-292-6 (pbk.)

I. Title.

PS8575.D618S44 2008   jC813'.54   C2008-904545-9

Kids Can Press is a **CORUS**™ Entertainment company

for Nancy, for her wisdom
and stories

CHAPTER 1

Wings

I opened my arms, leaned into the wind and fell up.

I wasn't surprised. I've had tons of flying dreams.

Usually I just flapped my arms really hard to lift off. Or ran with giant steps until they grew into man-on-the-moon bounces and finally I was floating above the houses. I'd dive forward with my shoulders and swoop up, each time getting higher and higher, using my hands out flat to steer left and right.

But this time my fingers were feathers. I had wings.

They were black. Not big and broad like crows' wings or narrow and pointed like seagulls'. They were short and rounded, like on those little brown birds you see everywhere.

I rose over the red rooftops (strange, I'd never noticed they were red), up over Main Street, the cathedral's twin spires, the flapping red maple leaf on the highest building on the highest hill. All of Antigonish spread out under me.

I sailed in a huge circle. I could see where the three rivers met the salt water, the big bump of forest that people called a mountain, the hospital, the golf course, the Trans-Canada Highway, the malls, and back around to the ocean.

Suddenly huge black clouds appeared out of nowhere. A nasty wind tried to rip my feathers off. Two crows blasted past, cawing loudly. They tucked into black arrowheads and dove for the safety of the trees. I tried to follow, but the wind knocked me upside down. I twisted hard right, straining every puny muscle in my thirteen-year-old body. Beneath me the university's red bricks flashed by, way too fast. Another hard twist. The fairground's red-roofed barn rushed toward me like a gigantic stop sign. I was going to crash!

Then I saw the riding ring. Soft sand. Yes! At the last second I saw the horse — a black horse with a rider dressed all in red.

"Look out!" I screamed. The black horse bolted sideways. The red rider fell. Down. Down. Head first. Thud. I screamed again — an empty, useless dream scream.

My yelp woke me up. Sunlight toasted the foot of my bed.

Something is wrong, said a little voice from a distant corner of my brain.

"Yeah. Flying dreams are supposed to be *fun*."

When I was little I thought flying dreams meant I

had some extra special talent, a future in the cockpit of a jet fighter or the space shuttle ... until I told my parents.

Dad said how much he had loved his flying dreams. Mom said that a lot of people with flying dreams had ESP, like Nanna. Dad told me to enjoy flying while I could because the dreams would stop when I grew up — when age became gravity and held me down. Then he said at least one in three people had flying dreams. I was perfectly normal.

Normal.

That was the last time I told them about any of my dreams.

Normal.

That was the problem.

Normal, normal, normal.

That was me — Ace of Average, King of Common, Master of Middle. I was so normal it made me sick. Just one of the herd, shorter than most of the girls in my grade, with feet two sizes too big and muscles four sizes too small. And my face — nose too wide, jaw too narrow — not ugly, but no girl ever looked my way.

Normal equals invisible. You'd think with a name like Frankie Uccello, genetics could have at least given me my father's dark Italian eyes and black curly hair. Girls loved black curly hair. But no-o-o, *my* hair was the same limp brown as all my mom's Scottish ancestors and my eyes were a boring grayish-brownish green.

Normal equals boring. I never made the best mark in any subject, never got a lead in a school play, never scored when the game needed it.

It wasn't like I didn't try. Dad signed me up for every sport and team activity designed to torture hopeless normals. But my total lack of success must have worn him down because last year, when I decided I wanted to skateboard, he never lectured me on how dangerous skateboarding was — he actually helped me buy a board! (As long as I promised I'd always wear a helmet, which reduced the chance of brain injury by eighty-five percent.)

Boarding was hard, *really* hard! Once I'd learned to stay upright most of the time, I liked it a lot. On a good day it was relaxing. Push, push, glide. Push, push, glide. Carving from side to side down a long slow hill. On a bad day it was stressful — when tricks I knew I knew, simple ollies and grinds, went bizarrely wrong and every window in every house watched me fail.

But I kept on practicing. The good days were so worth it. Even if it took me a month to learn what some guys could learn in a day, landing a trick was so cool. And fast downhill runs were really rippin'. Not that I did anything too crazy, like flinging myself off a flight of stairs. I knew my limits. I just wanted to have fun — and be able to do it again the next day.

After a year, I mastered the kickturn frontside and backside, could hold a manual for more than ten feet, ollie pretty darn high, grind curbs and do a passable kickflip. I learned the hard way *not* to get my board wet and let it stay wet. Rusty bearings lock. Board stops. Rider *doesn't*. I also learned how to fall without using my hands, get up and walk it off. And how the four kinds of bandages stocked in my backpack could be applied with just my teeth.

I often hung out with the other skaters when they practiced on curbs, steps or the convent's curved retaining wall with the sweet spot at one end. *They* never thought about getting hurt; they just rode. And offered tips to newbies like me, and never minded that I was totally normal with no real talent for skateboarding.

I had no real talent for anything. Normal also equals talentless. More than once I'd wondered if I was adopted — some leftover, bottom-of-the-barrel baby taken home out of pity — since the rest of my family is so crammed full of talent.

Mom can cook and sew and paint and fix the plumbing. Dad can take a car apart and put it back together on a weekend *and* build anything out of wood before you get out of bed on Monday morning.

And they both have the worst jobs parents could have. Did they plan it that way? Did my mom say, "Before our baby boy is old enough to be embarrassed by feet that are too big, a voice that cracks and squeaks, pimples, hair in new places and *everything* about girls, let's make sure he really understands embarrassed. Let's get jobs that'll make him an expert on embarrassed. Bob, you be a nurse, so when people ask, 'What does your father do?' they will forever correct him and say, 'Not your mother, dear. Your father.' And I'll be a teacher, *his* teacher — *three* different years! That ought to do it!"

It did. Then Mom got a provincial Teacher of the Year award and Dad got a Nova Scotia Excellence in Nursing award. People kept saying, "You must be so proud of your parents."

And if they weren't saying that, they'd be saying, "You must be so proud of your sister."

Bernie. Bernadette. Sixteen, tall, dark, curly-haired, beautiful, star basketball player, provincial prize winner in both chemistry and math, plays three musical instruments, speaks fluent French, and has boys calling her cell phone nonstop. It was like Bernie sucked up all the talent genes and left me with the broken mutant bits, not one talent, one special ability, one extraordinary thing to make me unique.

Until the night I dreamed I had wings.

CHAPTER 2

Late

I groaned and kicked the twisted blankets off my legs. The house was early-morning quiet. That didn't match the muffled sound of traffic and the angle of sunlight through my high basement window. My alarm clock blinked 4:43.

Wrong!

Where was my watch? I put it in my jeans pocket when I got home last night. I took it off to plaster my skinned wrist with bandages. I rummaged through the pile of once-worn clothes on the foot of my bed. I checked the twice-worn pile on the chair and the not-too-stiff-with-mud-yet pile on the floor. Not there, either.

I had visions of Mom, standing cross-armed in my doorway, rolling her eyes and saying, "Your sister washes her own clothes. You can't even get yours to the laundry room!" Or "I haven't seen your bedroom rug in so long I don't remember what color it is." Or "One of these days, I swear, *everything* on the floor goes in the garbage!"

Finally I spied some bloodstained denim. There! Under my Transworld Skating mags. I reached into the right-hand pocket. Nothing but a fist-sized hole. Oh, no! The left pocket — whew. My watch said 8:15.

"It's *LATE!*"

I opened my bedroom door and shouted up the stairs. "*IT'S LATE! IT'S EIGHT-FIFTEEN!*"

I jumped into another pair of jeans (no blood) and a long-sleeved T-shirt to cover the bandages. I staggered up to the bathroom, pulled my hair into a ponytail to hide the greasiness and painted some strong-smelling deodorant on my pits. No time for a shower. School started in twenty-five minutes. It took me at least ten minutes to get there. And I needed to eat.

Dad hollered from the upstairs hallway, "*POWER OUTAGE LAST NIGHT.*" A whining scream followed him down to the kitchen as he cranked the handle on his emergency radio. "*GET A MOVE ON, PEOPLE. IT'S SEVENTEEN MINUTES AFTER EIGHT!*"

He was just wearing jeans, his over-stretched moccasin slippers slapping the tiles. The hair on his chest, as curly as his head, was creeping down his slightly padded six-pack. It was going gray. I hadn't noticed that before. He looked *old*. Well, he *was* over forty.

"Is the power out at the school?" Mom called down. "Please tell me school's cancelled. Please tell me I can go back to bed."

I dropped some bread into the toaster. The elements glowed red hot. "Power's on."

Dad didn't hear me over the radio. "Big wind last

night took down trees all over the province," he reported loudly to Mom. "Radio says the Halifax area got hit really bad. Power's still out in half the city. Everyone's complaining about the power company. Nothing said about school closures."

"The power's back on," I repeated. "*Cook,* you stupid toaster!"

"Frankie! Never say stupid!" Dad scolded.

"It's a *toaster!* It doesn't have feelings."

Mom appeared, wearing a bright red sweater. There was something about that red.

Something is wrong.

"Yeah, if my freaking toast doesn't hurry up and cook, I'll be late," I growled.

"Frankie, stop talking to yourself." Mom spread her arms wide and ordered Dad, "Smug."

"Smug?" he asked, with a huge grin.

"A smooch and a hug."

"Only time for the old Pinch and Peck this morning." He squeezed and kissed and let go before he'd finished the sentence. "Power's back on."

"Shoot," said Mom. She poked his belly. "Tch, tch. Too many pineapple upside-down cakes in the hospital cafeteria."

"No, I think that's the chocolate-mint ice cream and the salt-and-vinegar potato chips."

"Honey, you have to learn some self control!"

"Keeps my mind off all those hot nurses."

"Bob!" She nabbed a chunk of his chest hair.

"*OUCH!*"

"Aren't you working today?"

"No. I'm taking an extra shift in orthopedics next week."

"You be careful about your back. Do you like my new sweater?"

"Did you *need* a new sweater?"

"I didn't need it. It was on sale."

Bernie came into the kitchen, pulling her long hair into a ponytail. Today her belly button wore a tiny green lizard. "Mo-om!" she said. "That sweater's so ... tight!"

"Hey, why should you young people be the only ones to show off? And *that* T-shirt's too *short!* And pull up your pants!"

"You never tell *him* to pull up his pants," she said, pointing at me. "He's the one who's going to break his neck tripping over his crotch. Mom, your sweater's way too red."

Mom ignored her. "Frankie, what do *you* think?"

"Red's all wrong for you," Bernie said. "It's too strong. Red is a power color. The color of anger. The color of —"

"Lo-o-ve," Dad crooned. He swept Mom into his arms for another quick kiss.

Bernie just kept on going. "Red is the color of the devil. The color of danger ... and emergency."

"Red-letter day," said Dad. He poured granola into a bowl.

Mom hugged her new sweater. "Red-carpet treatment."

"Seeing red!" Bernie snapped.

"Red sky at night, sailor's delight," said Dad, leering at Mom's chest.

"Red sky in the morning, sailor take warning," Bernie countered.

Dad loved a challenge. "Red herring."

"Red flag!" Bernie retorted.

Dad giggled. "Paint the town red!"

"Exit-sign red!" I ordered. This "red" thing was getting on my nerves.

The toaster popped. "Finally!" I grabbed the toast and danced the hot slices on my fingertips across to my plate on the opposite counter. "Ow, ow, ow!"

"You twerp," said Bernie. "You do that every morning. Why can't you put the plate next to the toaster?"

I slapped on some peanut butter and grape jelly and bit off half.

"Frankie, you didn't say what you think of my sweater."

I pointed to my mouth. "Mumph phull."

"I count on you," Mom pouted. "Maybe it's not my red. It *did* look different in the store. Those darn fluorescent lights."

She wasn't going to be happy until I gave my approval. It wasn't my fault I knew what looked good. "It's fine," I mumbled and took another bite.

"No, maybe Bernie's right. I better change."

I waved her to be still and jogged up to her room, to the scarf carousel that organized her huge collection — the carousel that was all *my* idea and *I* had planned to build her for Christmas, but she caught me measuring her closet and I had to tell her why and then she made Dad build it the very next weekend "because it had to be done right."

A black scarf with a silver border ordered "pick me." I brought it down and draped it over Mom's shoulder.

"Black and red. That's perfect!" Mom exclaimed. "Why didn't I think of it? You're so talented."

Talented. Sure. The Ace of Average has *one* talent — picking fashion accessories for his mom. I groaned. I shouldn't even know what "fashion accessories" means! If this was my only talent in life I might as well just throw myself off a roof.

"Don't get that look on your face," Mom said. "You know you're special."

It might be a parent's job to say things like that, but it didn't make it true. "Special is another word for retarded."

"No one uses that term anymore. It's called 'mentally challenged'."

"What's the difference? Lights on — no one's home. Two slices short of a loaf. Elevator doesn't go to the top floor. Lost a wheel on the wagon. That's me."

"Frankie, you have such an odd sense of humor."

Bernie said, "I'll be in the car."

"Not without breakfast," Mom ordered.

Bernie waved an apple in one hand and a granola bar in the other as the screen door slammed behind her.

"Do you want a ride?" Mom asked me.

"Nah." There was no room in Mom's Civic next to Bernie's mood. I scooped my homework off the dining-room table and stuffed it into my backpack.

Mom looked at my jeans. "If I can put up with those baggy, half-falling-off things, you could at least make sure they're clean. People are going to think I don't know how to do laundry."

"I couldn't find anything clean." I headed out the door.

"Did you look in the basket by your bed?" Mom shouted after me, a little shrilly. "If it was a bear, it would bite you!"

I picked up my board and helmet. Dad leaned into the garage. "Frankie, I forgot to tell you. Susan has this new physio program and she needed helpers so I signed you up. Be ready to go at ten after six."

"You did what? What if I don't want to?"

"Too late. They're counting on you."

"But I had plans!"

"Skateboarding isn't 'plans'. This'll be good for you," he said in his nurse voice. Then he added, "Tim signed up."

There was no time to argue. I'd be late for school. He timed it like that on purpose.

"Where's Bernie?" Dad asked. "I wasn't finished with Bernie." He spotted her in the waiting car. "I never got to 'red-hot lover'."

I threw down my board and hopped on.

"And 'red-blooded'!" Dad called in a deep, vampire accent as I leaned the turn onto the sidewalk. "I vant to drink your bl-o-o-d!"

CHAPTER 3

Red

Hawthorne Street ran downhill to Main between older, two-story family homes with fancy gingerbread trim and real painted-on colors — only a few were boring beige vinyl. We lived at the top of the steepest part of the street. That was a problem when I started skateboarding.

I carefully practiced on flat ground all last summer. But one morning as I was taping up the front of my board — it got split from too much puddle time — Dad asked, "Can you go downhill on that thing?" I didn't answer. He correctly took that as a "no" and asked why not. Mom said, "Don't think about it so much. Just do it. That's what boys do best. Not thinking. Just doing." I wasn't sure she was talking to me because she was staring at the back of Dad's head, cue-ball smooth since the hospital's cancer-prevention fundraiser the day before.

But she was right. I always over-thought everything. So that day I had gone straight out, hopped on my board, focused on the bottom of the hill and went for it. I was about halfway down, the board was my friend ... when I realized I had no idea how to stop! I dragged the sole right off of my sneaker, then bailed. Most of me made it to the bottom. Some skin decorated the concrete, and my knee bled like a waterfall.

I wore out three pairs of sneakers since then. But now I could cruise all the way to the traffic lights on Main with one push, riding the rhythm of the concrete blocks, *clack, clack, clack, clack, clack, clack.*

Except that morning.

An obstacle course of storm leftovers forced me to slalom slowly around lumps of leaves and branches, broken asphalt shingles, a twisted aluminum lawn chair, mangled flower baskets, a deflated kids' wading pool ... everything but kids. The sidewalk should have been full of kids heading for school, but except for a man in a motorized wheelchair weaving down the street — forcing cars to swing into the oncoming lane — I was the only person in sight.

Where were they? Were they still asleep? Was this Sunday? I checked my watch. Monday for sure. Whew, nothing dumber than going to school on a Sunday.

Most people already thought skaters were all dummies and dropouts. Sure, a lot of the guys didn't do so well in school and the RCMP knew many of them by their first names, but our skateboarding club had members from elementary school to university students and even two guys who owned their own computer business.

And then there was Graham, the only kid in ninth grade younger than me, but smarter than all of us put together — lazy but smart. Graham helped me learn my best trick, a one-eighty kickflip. He was a flatland artist, though he was as eager as the rest of us to test the ramps in the new skateboard park (if it ever got built).

The sun was already hot. The wet ground steamed. Autumn officially started next week, but summer wasn't giving up. Suited me fine.

The traffic lights turned yellow. I kicked up my board and stared at the street signs. Green with white letters — MAIN ST on top, AN T-SRÀID ÀIRD underneath. And at right angles, HAWTHORNE ST and SRÀID A'SGITHICH. I had no idea how to pronounce the Gaelic versions, but I bet they didn't sound anything like they were spelled.

The lights turned red — red eyes staring. I looked away, my heart suddenly racing.

Something is wrong.

"Will you shut up? Nothing's wrong. The storm is over. It's a gorgeous day."

Red.

Mom's sweater ... the rooftops in my dream ... the red rider.

That's when it finally hit me. I had a *color* dream! Finally! Another color dream!

It'd been nearly two years — two whole years since my last color dream — the turquoise dream ... the dream that started me thinking the impossible.

You see, my grandmother's favorite color was stuck-in-the-fifties turquoise. Turquoise vinyl dining-room set, couch and chairs. Faded turquoise bedspread and old winter coat with the fox collar. Dangly turquoise earrings. That was Nanna. And despite what happened, my turquoise dream was my all-time favorite dream.

I dreamed Nanna and I licked turquoise ice cream and rocked on a turquoise garden swing surrounded by beds of turquoise flowers under a turquoise sky. Rocking and smiling. Total bliss. Then she gave me a tight turquoise hug and kissed me good-bye. I woke up still feeling that hug ... and hearing my little voice whisper, *something is wrong.*

It followed all my color dreams. The yellow dream, the green one, the brown.

Something is wrong.

Of course something was wrong. All those other color dreams were *not* happy. Most of them woke me up with a shout and took months to forget. And I'll *never* forget the orange dream. Every horrid detail. Nine years later and it still made me sick to my stomach. The giant tree glowing orange — pulling me to it. To the orange house that swelled with orange fire, flames leaking from every window. And the orange girl standing on the scorched lawn, her arms black melted skin. And the screams.

But my turquoise dream was good. Happy. Beautiful. *Nothing* was wrong.

Three days later Nanna died. She had a stroke, slipped into a coma and never woke up.

Mom went off the deep end. There was still so much she had wanted to say to her mother. So much she had never asked. She should have seen it coming. She should have been there to say good-bye. *No one* got to say good-bye.

I did ... in my turquoise dream.

That's when I started to think the impossible — that I could dream the future! And that my other color dreams had been about the future, too. About things that happened in the days that followed. *Bad* things that I could have prevented, that I *should* have prevented.

After Nanna's funeral I figured if I ever had another color dream I would know it meant trouble, and I promised myself I would do something about it!

So ... a red dream. What did it mean? The red rider fell and hit his head ... or her head — I never saw the face.

The traffic lights blinked green. The crosswalk figure lit up and started counting down from twenty ... nineteen ... eighteen ... A car turned right on the red and blew his horn at me. "Hey, MY right of way!" I hollered and didn't speed up.

I never saw the face! Just the red rider falling from the black horse.

Fear galloped through my gut. *Tim* rode a black horse!

No, it couldn't be Tim! Tim didn't fall off horses. He was the best young rider in North Eastern Nova Scotia. That's what he said, and all the big ribbons pinned along the top of his bedroom bookshelf told the truth. He'd been riding ever since he got his pony, Jelly Bean, for his sixth birthday.

But that black horse he rode now — it was a long way to the ground from the top of that thing. If the fall didn't kill you, hooves the size of moons could make toe jam out of you in no time flat. I dropped my board and pushed uphill to ELM ST — SRÀID NAN AILM, the street with no elm trees.

But it must be Tim. Why would I dream about someone I didn't know? Tim was going to fall!

When? Where? I had dreamed about the fairgrounds. There was a horse show there on Saturday. Tim was going to have an accident at the horse show! It was up to me to save him!

But how could I when I was too scared of horses to go within ten blocks of one?

I'd have to keep Tim from going to the show. I had five days to make that happen. Five days? Five *years* wasn't enough. Tim *lived* for horse shows. He even quit the soccer team to train and show that black horse all summer!

I ollied off the curb to avoid a tree trunk sprawled across the sidewalk and the hood of some unlucky guy's Malibu. Way too much storm trash crowded the downhill slope, so I popped my board and hiked the rest of the way to school. There were lots more kids straggling in, and even though we were all late, everyone stopped to look around the schoolyard. Shredded strips of paper covered the asphalt, curbs, grass, red brick pillars and walls. Longer strips were snagged in the shrubs, fluttering like trapped birds.

The buses were late, too. They usually arrived way before me, even after being on the road for an hour or more while I was still sleeping. Man, I'd hate to live in the country.

Tim's bus pulled in and a bunch of noisy kids poured out. The smallest peeled off to the elementary school and the rest rushed indoors ahead of a scruffy, bony boy, Slug, the meanest kid in ninth grade and probably the whole province. He glared like he wanted to knock me over just because I was vertical. I slid my gaze to the bus, acting too cool to care. He grunted and clomped off in his unlaced work boots.

Thank God he wasn't in my class. Problem was, neither was Tim. We'd sat together since sixth grade. Now, our last year in Junior School, and we get split up.

Kim and Tim were the last two off the bus. Slug didn't seem to bother with them — which didn't make sense to me because in June they had tricked Slug out of that black horse. Sure Slug had stolen the horse — from his dad, of all people! Slug had planned on selling it at the livestock auction in Truro. The meat price was about six hundred dollars. Tim and Kim convinced Slug to give Kim the horse in trade for a really old baseball with some famous signature on it. Slug sold the ball on eBay for twenty-four hundred dollars! Sounds good, except Tim knew the horse was a purebred something-or-other and worth ten times that!

"The Great Horse Trade," Tim called it, because not only did they trade the horse for the ball, Kim also traded riding rights with Tim. She learned to ride on Tim's old pony, Jelly Bean, while Tim and the mega-expensive black horse won every horse show last summer.

At least that was Tim's version of the story, and Slug must have heard it because Tim had repeated it five thousand, four hundred and thirty-two times.

So I don't know why Tim was still in one piece ... unless Slug was still planning his revenge.

Kim nodded a shy hello to me. I blinked. I think it was the first time she had ever looked at me. "Hey," I replied. She was a seriously short seventh grader with blond hair a little longer than mine. Kind of cute but quieter than well-oiled ball bearings. It was hard to believe she had faced down Slug. She checked which way Slug went and went another way.

Tim appeared on the bus steps. I groaned out loud. He had on a red T-shirt ... dream-red. Tim was doomed.

He scratched his tight caramel curls as he looked around at the mess. "Holy freaking fish guts! Recycling plant blow up?"

I could feel sweat bead on my neck. "Ummm ... new shirt?"

"You like it?"

Stay calm. Stay calm. "Yeah, goes good with black." Tim called himself Black, even though he looked more like a long drink of double-cream coffee. I coughed to clear the awful tightness in my throat. "So, you're going to the horse show this weekend?"

Tim arched an eyebrow. "What do you care? You hate horses."

"I don't *hate* horses."

I didn't. Horses were beautiful creatures. Graceful. Powerful. More than once I had wondered what it felt like to ride all that power. But horses were also huge, with giant teeth and stomping feet and you never knew what they were thinking or when they would kick you or bite you or run you over. I might be one egg roll short of a combination plate but I was smart enough not to go near a horse.

Sweat dripped between my shoulder blades.

"The show was cancelled," Tim said. "A horse at the Fall Fair came down with strangles, and it might have infected the barns at the fairgrounds. That bug hangs around for ages."

"O-o-oh." I barely controlled a full-force sigh of relief. "Too bad."

"Sure is. That was the last horse-club show of the season. Only the Hug a Horse Halloween show left."

"There's another show?"

"Yeah, at Hug a Horse Farm. Why?"

"Are there any red roofs there?"

"Huh?"

"Are there any red roofs at Hug a Horse Farm?"

"No-o-o-o." He looked at me like I'd been playing hockey without a helmet. "Are you okay?"

My brain burned rubber. No horse show at the fairgrounds. The only one is in what, six weeks? Why dream about it now? And there were no red roofs there. So it couldn't be Tim who was going to fall. And I didn't know anyone else who rode a black horse. So it was just my hyperactive, sicko imagination. There was no red rider, no accident, no meaning to my dream. If I was any denser, light would bend around me. As if my color dreams meant something. As if I could see the future.

Trouble was, part of me was disappointed that Tim wasn't going to have an accident. How twisted was that? The finger of God should have come down and flicked me away. No loss. Lots more where he came from.

Flick.

CHAPTER 4

Garbage

"Hey, dude!" Graham hollered and whipped up on his board. He threw it into a power slide, halted in a low crouch, jumped up, spun his board in a three-sixty and plucked it out of the air with the precision of a juggler. "You'll never guess what I just bought!" he crowed. He ignored Tim. If you didn't have a board, you didn't exist.

The shining yellow of his board reflected off the bottom of his nose. "New board, eh?" I muttered.

He clearly expected a bigger reaction. He hunched over, fished an elastic from a knee-deep pocket and tied back his long brown hair. His chin sprouted a poor excuse for a beard — still, way more than most fourteen-year-olds could grow. "The Jesus look," Mom called it, though I'm sure Jesus didn't have purple streaks in his hair.

Mr. Billings, the vice-principal, shouted from the main entrance, "There will be NO skateboarding in the schoolyard before four P.M.!"

Graham grumbled, "Bucket-head," and gave me a dull, "Later, Frankie." He rode away across the parking lot.

"Yeah," I mumbled. "See ya."

"Frankie," Tim asked, heading in, "what's with you today?"

"*Nothing!*"

"You're supposed to wake up before coming to school."

"Yeah, well you're supposed to take your hat off in school." I smacked the hat off his head with a quick left jab and a flurry of pulled punches. I felt like hitting something for real. I kicked the blue recycle box in the foyer.

"Mr. Uccello! You have a problem?" Mr. Billings barked.

I slouched and kept on walking.

"Did that storm keep you awake all night, too?" asked Tim.

"Can't hear much in the basement," I said. I had an urge to tell him about my dream, but he wouldn't understand. Who would?

"Lighten up," said Tim. "It's Monday. Cannon blasts off today, as long as it doesn't rain."

True. Today was the day every kid looked forward to since entering sixth grade. Mr. Taylor, we called him Cannon, was the best teacher in the whole school. Some days he'd get so excited teaching science, he'd end up standing on his desk. And every September he'd take the ninth graders out to the soccer field and demonstrate the power of chemistry and household substances. Cornstarch exploded, iron filings burned, helpless fruit were launched into the ozone.

Cannon was the opposite of Bomb, short for Timebomb, our English teacher, a.k.a. Mr. Smith. No one ever knew when he was going to explode all over class and rant about social conscience or ethics or the environment or recycling or what some other class did wrong three days ago.

"See you at recess," said Tim, heading up the opposite hallway.

"Yeah, later." I stashed my gear in my locker and got to first period late but not last. A substitute teacher insisted on doing a detailed roll call: first names, middle names, the works. Reminding everyone of my *real* name.

Down the role she went. "Grade Nine A: Mary Alice Beaton? James Peter Bekkers? Lisa Lorraine Benoit? Yifru Tele Beyene?" She mutilated that one. Yifru didn't mind. He just beamed his blinding white smile and said, "Yes, I am also present, Miss," in his thick Ethiopian accent.

"Eleanor Ethel Cameron?" A few giggles over "Ethel" fluttered around the room.

Then on to the two Campbells, the three Chisholms and all the Macs. At John Angus Thompson I cringed. I was next.

"Frances Xavia Uccello?"

That was *not* my name! I had two options. I could make her read it right. Or I could speak up immediately before ...

"Is she here?"

Laughter.

I tried to say firmly. "It's *Frank*, Miss," but my voice cracked and what came out was "F...ank." The whole class roared.

"Oh, excuse me," she said. "I see it's Francis, is it? With an 'i'? Francis Xavier? Just like the University?"

I clenched my jaw and looked straight at the blackboard. The damage was done.

In next period, some boring DVD on community economic development put several kids to sleep and gave me too much room to think. Why had I wasted a second imagining I was special? I was just another dim bulb in the marquee of life. Even if I *could* dream the future, who could I tell? Who would believe me? Mom would go on about how brilliantly creative I was, and Dad would send me to a shrink or sign me up for another team sport. Being able to see the future was cool in movies and TV, but in real life you were just a wacko.

I glanced out the window. It was starting to rain. That meant no Blastoff. All I had to look forward to was some dumb volunteer work after school.

Why couldn't Dad leave me alone? I told him a million times things were fine — I was fine. Then he goes and signs me up for yet another chance to be useless, hopeless and totally embarrassed. Okay, that one bicycle rodeo was sort of fun. The little kids were a riot. Especially when little Michael popped off the side of the ramp straight into Sgt. Morris. The Mountie said he wasn't hurt, even though it was as clear as the double-sized nose on his face that he'd be talking in a high voice for a while. All the guys cringed and held their knees together, but no one felt sorry for Morris. He didn't like kids much — and he hated skateboarders.

And this idea of Dad's? What horror was next? Susan was a physiotherapist at the hospital where Dad worked. She was the tiniest grown-up I ever met, but God help you if you got in her way. She worked mostly with old people. Was I going to be helping old people? I had lots of experience. Nanna lived with us for five years.

At least Tim was signed up, too. Strange he didn't mention it.

The buzzer sounded. The hallways flooded with bodies trying to keep their personal space and still get to their next class. Suddenly a cross-current of Grade Nine D's forced two plastic grocery bags into everyone's hand. "Take this. Don't ask," a freckled boy ordered.

A voice boomed over the intercom. It was Timebomb. "Due to an unfortunate *incident* with the dumpsters, the next ninth-grade class has been postponed."

The hallways groaned long and loud.

"... will spend the next period and recess cleaning up the school grounds. Use the grocery bags, one as a glove, and one to collect the paper. Nine B and C will work out front. Nine A and D clean up the playground and the soccer field."

I met up with Tim and Mike. Mike was Tim's best friend. I got to know Mike last year when we formed a band for the talent competition. You'd never know looking at all that bred-in-the-bone muscle and farmer's tan that Mike was a talented musician. While I struggled to strum an electric bass — another of my less-than-great endeavors — and Tim fingered a decent lead guitar, Mike kicked butt on the sax. He got lots of time to practice because his dad found out the cows loved music, so he set Mike's music stand up in a corner of the milking parlor. The more Mike played, the more milk the cows gave. Next to his sax, Mike's favorite things in all the world were Holstein cows — oh, and Lana, a tall, dark-haired hotty in my class, too into horses and Tim to notice. Mike had a gift for the gab, too, though he never got to the point or the punch line. He just talked. Seemed his cows loved that, too. We never did find a drummer, so I had to keep the beat on my bass. I didn't totally stink, but we didn't come anywhere close to winning.

"Aren't you supposed to be out back?" Tim asked.

"With the Nine D's? You nuts?"

"Yeah, Slug and Paul in the same class — same county's bad enough!"

As we headed outside, Timebomb barked, "Uccello! *Back* door!" and marched all the Nine A's and D's to the playground. Warm drizzle drifted in from the south, melting the paper and making it next to impossible to pick up. Not that many kids tried. Most milled around and complained forty or fifty times that Cannon's launch would be cancelled. They talked and laughed and used the bags in creative ways to keep dry. A few environmentally aware do-gooders who had figured out the grocery-bag-as-a-glove thing had their other bags full and were collecting new bags from the teachers.

The day just got wetter and grayer. Bomb herded kids around, as useless as a Chihuahua yapping at cattle. A lot of the paper actually disappeared, some into bags, but more ground into a gray pulp on the pavement and grass. The buzzer sounded for recess. A few sixth graders who didn't seem to care that it was raining came out and played on the swings.

Colors popped in the wet. Greens shone greener, blues bluer. Then it occurred to me that from where I stood I could also see browns and tans and pinks and purples, lots of purples — but *no* red. Not a ball cap or collar or stripe on a sneaker. Over eighty people in the schoolyard and not a speck of red. The total opposite of my dream. Way too strange to be a coincidence, right?

No! My dream was just a dream. "Enough's enough," I growled. A nearby kid dropped his half-full bag of paper bits and scurried away.

A few minutes later someone got the bright idea to explode their grocery bags. They twisted the ends tightly and stomped on them. *Bang! Bang! Bang!* Timebomb charged into the ruckus. The crowd parted. And there, on the far side of the playground, at the edge of the soccer field, was red.

A red jacket.

A *dream-red* jacket.

Its wearer turned and looked straight at me. It was Maura-Lee Chisholm. Weird Maura-Lee.

Of all the kids in my grade, I carefully avoided three. Slug was clearly top of the list. Then Paul, over-muscled and recently over-interested in gas and matches — a danger to himself and all of North Eastern Nova Scotia.

The third was Maura-Lee. Ever since second grade, when she and I stayed in during recess to finish coloring our life-size figures — you know, you lie down on a huge piece of paper and the teacher draws a line around you. I took a long time because I had no talent for coloring inside the lines. Maura-Lee was fussy, adding so much detail that hers looked alive. But when she finished, she colored the face a dark gray. Then she started coloring all the other paper faces. Pinks and purples. Greens and blues. She'd colored most of the class before Mrs. Cook came in, took one look and got really angry. Her face turned bright red. So did Maura-Lee's, and she kept shouting, "I did it right! I did it right!"

I've been avoiding Maura-Lee, Weird Maura-Lee, ever since.

So there she stood. Wearing the only red in sight and staring straight at me. More like straight through me. I swear if you stood behind me you'd see daylight through the holes. I had to move.

A loud hoot of laughter jumped from behind the south wall of the school. It wasn't nice laughter; it sounded like Paul.

"Throw it over here!" Paul shouted.

I admit the shout pulled me as much as Maura-Lee's stare pushed. And as Nanna used to say, "Better the devil you know than the devil you don't." I walked around the south corner of the building.

"I said throw it over here," Paul repeated. He and four boys stood in a loose circle looking down at a black lump of garbage.

"I ain't pickin' it up," said a bulky boy. He was new, but I didn't need an introduction to know I should steer clear of him. The boy nudged the black lump of garbage with his toe. "I think it's still alive."

He was right. The garbage had eyes. Tiny beadlike eyes. It lay on its side, shivering. One small web foot paddled, trying to grip the pavement. The tiny claws caught. It struggled to stand, but flopped back, hopelessly snatching the air with quick outspread wings ... black wings ... short and round.

My wings.

CHAPTER 5

Injured

I heard a scuff of gravel behind me. I felt the red of the jacket before I turned my head and saw Maura-Lee out of the corner of my eye.

"Kick it over here, then," Paul ordered again.

"It's not dead."

"I can fix that." The four boys laughed.

A deep rumble of a large engine vibrated off the brick wall. The dark brown bulk of the garbage truck rolled into view, heading for the dumpsters. It started to swing around the circle of boys, then stopped. The passenger window powered down and the driver leaned past a massive Rottweiler.

"What's that you have there?" the driver shouted.

No one answered. They backed all the way around the building, never taking their eyes off the truck driver's face. It was the face from a horror movie — only this face was real. It looked like the left side had been erased, or encased in a smooth, pinkish-white putty with features stiff and out of focus.

I glanced around. Maura-Lee had vanished. I wanted to vanish, too. Here was The Man with Half a Face, the man they say had burned down his house and killed his whole family. And gotten away with it. But I was chained to the spot, to the shivering black bit of life on the shiny wet ground. It had just confirmed, without a doubt, that I *did* have one true talent. There were no eurekas, no cheers, no bells ringing out. Just silent, intense knowing.

I had dreamed this bird. I had *been* this bird. Torn from the black sky on those black wings to swoop past the black horse ... of course, it *was* a color dream.

But not a *red* dream ... a *black* dream! And something *was* wrong. Right there at my feet.

"Is it alive?" the garbage man asked.

I flinched, trying not to think about the face, the stories. I nodded.

"Then you'll need this." He fiddled with something on the seat of the truck and climbed down from the cab. Light glinted from his right gloved hand — the thin sharp blade of a Swiss Army Knife. He raised the blade and drove it into the side of the dark green shoebox he held in his other hand. He reamed out a row of small holes and passed the box to me. I wondered if his hands were buried in scars like his face. I wondered if he deserved those scars.

"This'll do the trick," he said. "Looks like a storm-petrel. The first twenty-four hours are the most critical with injured birds. Keep it dark and quiet. Give it water, and if it doesn't die of shock before tomorrow it might make it. Good luck." He climbed back into the truck. His Rottweiler laid its cinder-block head on the dash and waited for the view to change. They rumbled over to the dumpsters.

I looked at the box, at the bird. I knew about shock. I had tried saving four baby birds. Yellow-cornered bills begging endlessly for food. Until they died. Mom always said I should have let nature take its course — there was a reason they were abandoned, they were going to die anyway and I only prolonged the agony. And added mine to it.

Even though she was probably right, I never stopped trying. But I had no talent for fixing baby birds. And every tiny death left a big hole. Every hope of a bird growing up and flying free ended in a handful of cold feathers.

And here was another failure waiting to crush me. But this time I had no choice.

I had dreamed this bird, and I was going to do whatever it took to see it spread those beautiful black wings and fly away.

The buzzer for the start of class startled me. I took the cover off the shoebox. It smelled strongly of egg sandwiches. I gently cupped my fingers around the dark feathers and placed the bird in the box. It lay quietly, head skewed to one side, eyes shut. I closed the lid and carried the box around to the back of the school. I tucked it under a little round shrub, one of a dozen crowded in a patch of bark mulch behind a short picket fence. No one would notice it there.

What did the garbage man call the bird? A petrel? I'd have to look that up.

I followed the Nine A's from class to class, but my mind was never where my feet were. It was out under the bush ... or in the dark sky, flying, flying.

A steady drizzle gloomed out the morning. At lunch Tim got dragged off by a seventh grader he knew from Hug a Horse Farm, where he did all his riding. She insisted he help her with a story for the school paper. Tim was happy to go because someone actually wanted his opinion. Or, Mike said, because she was cute. Tim always attracted the good-looking girls — Tim and horses ... or maybe it was horses first and then Tim — Mike wasn't sure which.

We hung out in the cafeteria and gazed out the huge front windows, watching the rain melt the last of the paper pieces. Mike whined about not getting to watch the girls show off their summer tans.

I shrugged. "My mom says tanning makes wrinkles and moles. They'll all look like prunes by the time they're thirty."

"Who kicked you in the head today?" asked Mike. "I *like* tans. Pale skin makes me think of winter. I hate winter."

"Yeah." The green box would be getting wet and cooled by the wind. The bird needed heat.

Mike went on about Lola, his favorite cow, who had given birth to healthy twin heifers (that's girl calves — and in the milking business, that's good). And how he'd been up half the night with his dad because the wind had taken the roof off the tractor shed and the flapping steel sheets scared the herd into the woods. His dad was afraid they'd be injured with so many branches and trees down. But when the cows came in to milk, there were just a few cuts and bruises to clean up.

I considered telling him about the petrel, but he never gave me a chance. On and on he gabbed. Something about chainsaws and barbed wire and bears. I stopped listening altogether when I saw the red jacket coming through the front doors of the school. What was Maura-Lee doing out in the rain? No one else in ninth grade went out. No one else was that weird. Maura-Lee broke all the rules.

Not the teachers' rules ... the *real* rules. Like "Don't let anyone know how smart you are." When I got a super-rare A on a test, I never told my friends.

And Maura-Lee? Well, she didn't brag. Actually, the only time she said *anything* was to answer in class — correctly. And every year she built the winning science-fair project, so the whole school knew Maura-Lee had brains to burn.

And the rule "Be yourself but never stick out." Maura-Lee stuck out. Her hair changed color like a chameleon in a jelly bean factory and she wore any-thing from priss to punk. Totally unique. Except that day Mary Alice had on the identical honey-yellow shirt over dark brown tank top and pants. I wouldn't have noticed if Mary Alice hadn't screamed when she came face-to-face with Maura-Lee and the number one girls' rule: "Never ever wear exactly what someone else is wearing." Mary Alice was so upset she went home at recess and changed.

And then there was the "all eighth-grade girls are evil" rule. (Okay, this was my personal rule.) Eighth grade girls knew what effect they had on eighth-grade boys. No wonder I had the worst marks of my life last year. And ninth grade didn't look like it was going to be much better. How was I supposed to concentrate with those curves in tight clothes? And the way they smiled at boys and tossed their hair and wiggled and pretended they were nice — when they weren't. All they wanted was to make us look at them, and then they'd look at each other like they knew what we were thinking and they'd giggle. Only they didn't know what *I* was thinking. Well, maybe a little, but the rest was my secret. Not one of them knew how much I hated that giggly stuff. Not one of them was worth more than the look they stole from me.

At least Maura-Lee wasn't like that. She never giggled. She was quiet ... and alone — breaking the biggest rule of all: "Never be seen standing alone." Maura-Lee was always by herself — in the schoolyard or cafeteria. She was Weird Maura-Lee. And kids said she could read minds.

CHAPTER 6

Secrets

Yup, that's what they said. Maura-Lee could read minds. They'd been saying that since elementary school. You can't believe everything you hear, but something like that sticks. Especially when the I-am-superior girls kept repeating it.

The end-of-lunch buzzer blasted away my thoughts. Only two more periods and I could see if the bird was still alive.

Bomb's class was last. We all endured a rant about vandalism and bad morals due to violent video games. I tuned out and planned how I'd hang around after school without being obvious, wait for the place to empty out before retrieving the petrel. I'd take it home, put it in my closet and close that door *and* my bedroom door — two closed doors between the bird and Mom's cat, Pookey. I'd get the bird a dish of water and keep an eye on it.

Then I remembered the volunteer thing.

At the last bell, I bolted for my locker, grabbed my

stuff and ran out back. At least the rain had stopped. The sky was white with dapples of thick blue-gray. The sun promised to shine soon. The smell of fried chicken and grilled burgers blew in from Fast-food Alley two blocks away. Tim was halfway along the lineup of yellow buses.

I shouted to him, "So what's going on tonight?"

"Huh?"

"Dad volunteered me for something. Said you were signed up, too."

Tim flashed a grin. "Physiotherapy. For kids, mostly. It's really cool." The bus doors creaked, threatening to close without him. He leaped aboard. "See you at 6:30!"

The bus pulled away. I watched his face in the window. He kept grinning that grin — the spitting image of Pookey when she ate Dad's goldfish.

If I was brighter than a burned-out lightbulb, I'd have started worrying then and there, but I had something more urgent on my mind.

When I was the only one around, I wandered to the south end of the school. A few little kids played in the puddles behind the elementary school next door. I could see the corner of the shoebox, still planted under its shrub. I stepped over the picket fence. My heart started pounding.

What if the bird was dead? Cold and stiff and awaiting burial in the dumpster? It would be sad ... but easier.

I slid the box cover open a crack. One tiny eye blinked, then closed tightly against the light. The bird's head drooped down till its beak touched the cardboard.

Did it wonder if I was about to eat it? Was it submitting to its fate? Was it too exhausted to care?

Something blue under the bird's right wing caught my eye. I reached in and pushed back the damp feathers. A blue hot/cold gel pack, still warm.

That's why Maura-Lee had been out in the rain!

Three thoughts flashed through my mind: *Brilliant — why didn't I think of that?* And *How dare she? This is my bird!* And *Maura-Lee had definitely been watching me earlier.* I looked around. A creepy feeling crawled down my spine. I cradled the shoebox under my arm and sped for home.

In my bedroom, I examined the petrel closely. I carefully opened each wing. The thin, fragile bones and itty-bitty muscles resisted with surprising strength. Nothing seemed broken. Its right foot paddled against the box in protest. I didn't like the way its left toes stayed clenched tight. Then I saw a small pale gray spot on the back of the petrel's head where the black outer feathers were missing. It must have hit its head. That's why its balance was screwed up. It had a concussion.

I had a concussion once. "Used my head," Mom said. "Don't do it again!" I slipped or tripped, I'm not sure which because I still can't remember ten minutes on either side of the accident. I was running down the stairs on Christmas morning. The next thing I knew I was looking at the dead flies in the front hall light fixture. Dad had his hands on either side of my neck and was telling me not to move. Mom was saying to someone on the phone, "Of course I know it's Christmas! No. We can't bring him in ourselves. He might have a broken neck! My husband's a nurse. No, my husband. He says we can't move him ..." And the snippy old nurse at the hospital — one of those sad people who get to work on Christmas — kept asking me if the room was spinning or if I was spinning and I kept asking her, "What's the difference?" I thought it was funny, but Dad got mad and made me answer. I said the room was spinning and I felt like I was going to fall over. That meant I had a concussion. I was okay after a day of sleeping and barfing.

The petrel probably thought the box was spinning. It would be okay in a day or two. Then it would spread those wings and sail high into the sky. And it would have *me* to thank for it. *That's* why I dreamed this bird. To save it and send it soaring.

I breathed a huge sigh of relief. I *knew* I was doing the right thing. I bet this was just like the feeling Nanna used to get when she "knew" who was on the phone when it rang. "I don't see why you need that call-display thingy," she'd tell Dad. "If you just paid attention, you'd know who was calling." Well, I was paying attention this time, Nanna. I was going to save the petrel.

But first I had to treat it for shock. I hauled a cardboard box out of the recycle bin in the garage, lined the bottom with newspapers and put it in my closet. Then I filled a hot water bottle — not too hot — put it in the box and propped the little bird against it. A water bowl went in next. I dipped my finger into the water and placed a drop on the petrel's beak. The water seeped in between the upper and lower bill. The bird didn't react. I dripped some more. No response. Maybe it would drink if I left. I closed the closet doors. Nothing else I could do ... except worry.

Mom got home at 5:30. "Anyone else for chowder?" She must have had a bad day. Fish chowder was Mom's favorite comfort food. I hated fish. She knew, but she still asked. I put a frozen pizza in the microwave. By 6:00 Dad still hadn't made it home. Since I'd done my home-work in study period, I planned an evening jumping the concrete stairs behind the Credit Union. But at 6:05, Dad roared up on his old Honda Goldwing, tossed his helmet on the kitchen counter, grabbed a piece of pizza and Mom's keys and barked, "Frankie, time to go."

Dad never talked much while driving — had to con-centrate on the road, he said — but that evening he talked a *lot*. "Get off my tail! Where'd you buy your license? Maniac! The sign says keep right! Can't you read?"

There was obviously something bugging him. "So where are we going?" I asked carefully.

"Meadow Green." He growled at the vehicle ahead of us. "Can you drive any slower?" End-of-season tourists — old people in a really big RV doing dumb stuff in slow motion — had backed up traffic so bad some genius behind us decided to pass where he shouldn't. Tim lived in Meadow Green. I assumed we were going to pick him up.

The Trans-Canada slowed at the intersection to St. Andrews — a scary piece of highway where local drivers leaving businesses, gas stations, restaurants and hotels try not to get smacked by huge trucks ignoring the lower speed limit. Dad had seen more than his share of accident victims from that very intersection in the ER. Once we got past it, into forests and farms and soft, rolling hills, he would usually relax, but not this evening.

He ranted at the tractor weaving its fully loaded hay wagon over both lanes until it turned off at a big dairy farm, at the kids on bicycles riding without helmets, at the potholes and piles of loose gravel on the Meadow Green road. He was ready for a fight. Like the day he took his Goldwing for a tour and forgot to call to say he'd be home late. Or the day he left the back door open and Pookey ran away. Times when Mom would be scared or mad or both and he'd come home knowing he'd done something wrong and was already angry, ready for a fight.

We drove along Meadow Green's harvested fields and pastures bordering the river hidden by trees, then up into dark green woods again. Then *past* Tim's yellow house.

"I thought we were going to Tim's!"

"You thought wrong."

The dirt road forked. When we went right, I knew where we were going. And I knew what the fight was going to be about.

Horses.

We were going to Hug a Horse Farm.

Chapter 7

Dancing

"I'm not going near a horse."

Dad clenched his jaw and stared straight ahead. "This will be good for you."

"I'm not doing it!"

Dad drove steadily up the driveway between two long, green pastures.

Though I hadn't been to Hug a Horse since I was seven, I remembered the board fence running along the driveway like a giant rainbow, deep purple, then blue, green, yellow, orange and red. At the top, the driveway split — left to the owner Vanessa's low brick house between a little apple orchard and gardens of giant sunflowers. On the right, the driveway ran up a steep bit to the outdoor riding ring with its faded white fence, the big dark brown barn beyond and the huge steel arena behind that. Tim and Kim stood by the barn. Tim waved.

Dad had planned it well. How could I make a scene in front of Tim? Let him see what a wuss I was? And

Kim, who could stand up to the county's biggest bully? I was trapped.

Dad turned the car at the house and stopped. "Get out."

I didn't. Panic beat in the pit of my stomach. I felt dizzy.

"Susan will drive you home," said Dad, his voice like concrete.

I took several quick short breaths. "And you told her I was *afraid* of horses."

"What sort of father do you think I am?"

"A father who cared about how I felt would be nice."

"For Pete's sake, one little thing ten years ago. Get over it."

"*Seven* years ago. And it wasn't *one little thing!* Being run down by a team of giant horses is NOT *one little thing!*"

"You were *not* run down. Your mother pulled you out of the way. You were just scared, that's all. Now's your chance to stop being scared."

"I'm not scared ... I'm ... I'm cautious. Horses are dangerous!"

"I'm sure these horses aren't or Susan wouldn't be able to use them. Now get out."

I did. A blast of wind slammed the car door behind me. Not my fault, but the loud thud felt good. Dad glared at me and took off.

Tim walked over, scuffing gravel with his big sneakers and grinning that grin. This was a great joke to him. I wanted to strangle him.

"Hey, Frankie," said Tim. "Come meet the gang."

"You never said I'd have to work with horses. You know I don't know anything about horses."

"You don't have to. All you have to do is walk along and make sure the rider is safe."

"How would I know safe? Horses are ... horses are ..." Totally, freaking terrifying. "What if I can't do it?"

"Then we'll have to tell Joey."

"Joey?"

"Yup. He'll be here in a few minutes. You're his siderunner."

"*My* Joey?"

"Double yup. That's who this program is for," said Tim. "Joey, and people like him. Therapeutic riding is for the handicapped, or challenged, or whatever's politically correct. It's a nationwide thing. Susan and Vanessa set up the program here last year. Being on horseback makes you use a ton of little muscles to help keep your balance. It's super physiotherapy. And the contact with the horses — it's amazing what it can do for the head." He paused for a breath. "Joey came last week but he wouldn't get on the horse."

"Smart kid."

Joey was eight and had autism. I was his baby-sitter. He mostly sat cross-legged in the middle of the living room rug, endlessly rocking and waving his hands in the air. It was a pretty easy job — as long as I didn't ask him to do something he didn't want to do. Then he could shout "AAH, AAH, AAH" for three hours straight! No ear plugs on the planet could keep you sane through one of Joey's tantrums.

Last spring (my third time at Joey's), Pookey snuck out of our house and tailed me to his house. She sat outside Joey's front door, yowling to get in. Joey stopped rocking, got up and went to the door. The moment they saw each other it was love at first sight. Joey sat on the floor and Pookey climbed into his lap. She curled into a ball, nose under her paws, purring like a tiny two-stroke engine. They both stayed still as statues until Joey's parents came home. When I picked up Pookey to take her home, Joey said, "Bye-bye, pretty kitty." That would be sort of cute except that Joey hadn't spoken a clear word since he was four! I thought his mom was going to pass out! So, ever since, Pookey comes baby-sitting with me. And Joey has started talking and interacting with the world in lots of different ways.

"They figured with *you* here," said Tim, looking a little apologetic, "Joey would get on the horse."

"Joey does what Joey wants."

But I was stuck. If they told the poor kid I'd be here, I *had* to help or there'd be hell to pay the next time I went to baby-sit. AAH, AAH, AAH. Forget it.

A gritty rumble came from the barn as the tractor-sized door slid open. Lana and Patsy stepped out, the two hottest girls in the whole school — the last two nails in my coffin. "Come on, you guys," Lana called. "Time to get ready."

Tim headed up the slope. I could barely breathe. "Yoga breaths, yoga breaths," Nanna used to say when I woke from a bad dream. I wished I could wake from this one. I tried breathing with my belly. My queasy stomach said that was *not* a good idea.

I followed Tim. The wind hissed through a row of pines at the far end of the riding ring. I wrapped my hoodie tight, trying not to shiver out loud. Still no horses in sight. They must be in the barn — the barn I was getting too close to.

Lana flashed her perfect white teeth at Tim. She was tall (almost as tall as Tim) with short wavy brown hair and a model's figure. She was always flirting with Tim, which really annoyed Mike. "I didn't know you liked horses, Frankie," she said. Her expression said, "I like people who like horses."

I swallowed and straightened up as much as my stomach would allow. "Horses are cool."

"Sure are," said Patsy. She was capital P pretty, but high-maintenance pretty. Blond and burgundy streaks in her molasses brown hair, precisely applied makeup, designer clothes. "I'll go call them," she said and disappeared inside.

Tim dragged the door wide open. A gust of wind swirled a knee-high tornado of dust straight at me. I put my hand to my nose, wincing at the stink about to gag me ... but there was no smell! Or horses. The low sun stretched our shadows halfway down the wide concrete aisle lined with big horse stalls, all golden-yellow stained wood with brass name plates ... and all empty.

Lana gave me a suspicious look. I faked a cough. "Umm, where are the horses?" I asked, ever so casually, ever so fake.

"Oh, they don't live in here anymore," she said. "They live outside now. It's *much* healthier for them. We only take them in when we need them."

Patsy walked to the open back door, gated by two thick boards. "Come O-on." she hollered in a clear sing-song voice. I felt the drumming hooves before I heard them. I stepped backward. All my blood drained to my feet.

Control! Control! Don't let them see your fear!

Tim saved my life. "Come on, Frankie. There's some stuff you're supposed to read before we get started."

I barely crushed the urge to run. I walked with Tim to the arena. Behind us the thunder of hooves suddenly stopped. Laughter trickled out of the barn.

We walked through monster sliding doors into a space big enough for two halfpipes end to end — not that you could skateboard on the sand floor. As my eyes gradually adjusted to the softer light from the clear roof panels, I could make out two sets of homemade wooden bleachers right in front of us. Tim dragged a trunk out from under one, opened it and passed me several sheets of paper stapled together.

"No need to memorize it," he said. "Susan will tell you exactly what to do, but you might as well wait in here. The barn gets a little hectic when we get the horses ready, and you'll just be in the way."

I nodded and took a deep breath. The pounding in my ears eased off.

A soft *thunk* from the far end of the arena made me look up. That's when I saw the black horse. It was walking around with *no* collar, *no* rope — *no nothing!* And the only thing between that horse and me was a thin yellow rope tied between the two bleachers. My heart stopped.

I judged the distance to the door. Could I escape before the horse got this far? I glanced at Tim. He just stood there, watching the beast. Then I saw a girl on the other side of the horse. With the distance and the dimness I couldn't make out her face. I held my breath, waited for her to catch the beast. Only she didn't. She raised her arms. Her hands seemed to be signaling something. Not "Get out of the way" or "Run for your life." No, all her attention was on the horse. And the horse's on her. She said, "T-r-r-rot!" and walked in a little circle and the horse trotted around her. When she stopped moving, so did the horse. It turned its thick, arched neck and looked at her. She called, "Walk on," and it did. It went wherever she went — left, right, backward. It looked like dancing, like the girl was dancing with the horse.

Then the horse trotted straight into the far corner, spun around and went in the opposite direction.

"Oops," Tim said. "She missed that."

"Missed what?" I was on my toes like a sprinter in the blocks.

"His body language," Tim replied. "He said 'No, I don't want to go this way any more.' He stopped bending, put his weight on his inside shoulder and stiffened his neck. She needed to push a little harder right then. He took advantage of her and went right instead of left. He's probably right-handed, so that's easier for him. Funny, most horses I know are left-handed."

"Oh," I said, pretending I understood.

Patsy and the seventh grader from the school paper came up behind us.

"Hi, Michelle," said Tim. "This is Frankie."

I gave her a quick nod, afraid to take my eyes off the black horse. But I relaxed a teeny bit. Two more bodies between me and it. Safety in numbers. Still, I needed to know. "If there's no rope, how come the horse doesn't just leave?"

"Neat trick, huh?" said Tim.

"It's no trick," said Michelle. "She's told him that she's the boss horse by the way she moves. He has to follow. The boss is always the leader. It's called 'natural horsemanship' — no fancy equipment to force the horse to obey. But she's amazing: he's her first horse, and she's only been at it for a few months."

"It takes most people years to learn what a horse is thinking," said Tim.

"It's almost like she can ... well, you know."

"Yeah," Tim replied.

"All that natural stuff is just a fad," said Patsy. "Horses got trained just fine before that came along."

"It's not new," Michelle said stiffly. "It just got lost when humans started to industrialize the planet and make horses into machines and tools for their own pleasure and got in too much of a hurry to think about what was important for the horse and —"

"Yeah, whatever," said Patsy. She asked Tim, "Do we really need to put the neck straps on today? We're not doing any trot work."

"Susan insists we put them on anyway."

Michelle gave Patsy an I-told-you-so look, and they went back to the barn. The girl in the arena put a collar on the horse's head and led him toward us. I stepped quickly behind one of the bleachers. Not just because the horse was getting so close. I could make out the girl's face.

It was Maura-Lee.

Again.

CHAPTER 8

The Riders

How can you avoid someone for so many years, and then *bam,* in your face — three times in one day? Coincidence?

"There are no coincidences," Nanna used to say. "Just intentions of fate. Pay attention to intentions."

Don't worry, Nanna. I will.

Maura-Lee unhooked the yellow rope and looked over at me. I looked down at the papers I hadn't read.

Tim said, "Better get a move on, Maura-Lee. The others are almost ready."

"It only takes seven minutes to put on his tack," Maura-Lee replied tightly, and they were gone.

Tim picked up a stack of orange pylons and started pacing off the arena, setting down pylons in precise patterns. I sucked in a shaky breath. I had no clue what to do. If it wasn't for Joey, I'd be hitching for home that very moment. Instead I climbed to the top of the bleacher and stared at the papers.

The first page had some history of hippotherapy. Sounded like riding hippos. I'd have to look that word up. "Riders learn a new skill, improve motor control, extend attention span and, most important, gain self-esteem. This activity is also an enjoyable way to meet new people and make new friends." Sure. There was some stuff about how it helped people in wheelchairs, those with cerebral palsy, developmental delay, Down's syndrome and autism.

"Those with autistic tendencies," it said "sometimes interact better with the unconditional nature of animals" — Pookey was proof of that — "but have to be supervised closely so they do not become overwhelmed by too much stimulation and act out inappropriately." Great. Joey's AAH, AAH, AAH tantrums would not go over real well!

One page listed guidelines for volunteers. A list of do's: be prompt, reliable, wear suitable clothing, listen to the instructor and *smile.* I chewed my lip. Smile — yeah, right.

Then the list of don'ts: don't chat, don't invite visitors to watch — respect the riders' privacy.

A silver Saturn and an old faded-red Mazda pulled up outside the arena door. A woman and girl got out of each vehicle. The girls had the same thin brown hair, full cheeks and slightly slanted-up eyes. Down's syndrome. They energetically dragged their mothers over to the barn.

Deep breaths. Deep breaths. I read some more. "The leader's job is to be at the horse's head and be in control of the horse. The purpose of the siderunner is to ensure the safety of the rider, to hold the rider's leg or waist strap if told to and walk or jog beside the horse." *Beside a jogging horse!* No way!

"In case of emergency, where a rider fall appears probable, the siderunner attempts to catch the rider to prevent or soften the fall." Emergency? I imagined the horse suddenly going crazy. How could I catch the rider *and* run for my life?

"Hi, Frankie!" Susan swept in the door, a yellow ball cap on her cropped black hair. Her tiny size and tight, bouncing stride reminded me of a Jack Russell terrier. Behind her came a complete opposite human being — round and calm, with a smile that made me smile despite my misery.

"Vanessa, this is Frankie, Bob Uccello's son."

"Hi, Frankie. You're a friend of Tim's, right? I believe we met some years ago."

"He's going to get Joey Gillis on a horse tonight," Susan announced.

"Look," I said. "I don't think —"

"No need to be humble," Susan said. "Ever since you taught Joey how to make his own lunch and do the dishes, Mr. Gillis can't stop raving about you."

"But Joey learned that stuff by himself."

"Couldn't have done it without you, Frankie. You will make a wonderful therapist some day. Hope you're keeping your marks up. You'll need good marks to get into university." Susan barely took a breath. "Did you read that handout? Good, then I don't have to explain things."

Tim finished placing pylons and headed our way.

Lana and a younger, blond and freckled girl walked in.

"Hi, Lana. Hi, Margaret," said Susan. "Where are the others?"

"Right behind us," Lana answered.

A small parade entered the arena. Maura-Lee with her black horse, now saddled, Michelle and Kim, each leading a yellow-brown beast, and Patsy pulling a rust-red pony with black legs. I ducked behind Susan and Vanessa. My mouth went dry. My chest felt like one of those horses was already sitting on it. The yellow-brown horses were even bigger than Maura-Lee's.

"Warm them up," Susan barked.

Tim translated. "We need to move the horses around a bit to get their back muscles used to the saddle. Then we can tighten the girth. That's the strap that holds the saddle on."

"I know what a girth is. I'm not *retarded*," I grumbled, just as the girls with Down's and their mothers came into the arena. My face got red hot. I wished I could have stuffed the word back in my mouth.

One of the girls smiled a happy, big-toothed smile and said in a booming voice, "I'm Mary. I'm ten plus one. How old are you? What's you name?"

Susan said, "Mary, this is Frankie. He'll be working with Joey."

"Mary is quite a conversationalist," said Vanessa. "Mary, you'll be riding Maura-Lee's horse, Prince. And Tim and Kim will be your siderunners."

"I good at riding horses," Mary said to me. "I can gallop fast! I ride Fur. I like Fur. Do you like Fur? Do you like macaroni and cheese? I like you hair. It like girl's hair. You pants are falling down."

"Mary," Susan ordered. "You're riding Prince today."

"NO!" said Mary. "I ride Fur!" She crossed her arms. A large Halloween-pumpkin grimace pulled down her mouth.

"Joey is riding Fleur today," Susan said firmly.

Mary's lower lip started to tremble.

Vanessa said in a soft voice, "Mary, Prince was looking forward to you riding him today."

A bright yellow Beetle drove up and a woman in her early twenties got out. She fished two crutches from the back seat and swung toward us, metal braces on each leg.

"Hi, Ellen!" Mary called. "I ride Fur today."

Susan groaned and shook her head at Mary's mother, who just shrugged helplessly. The four horses lined up in front of the bleachers. The horse Michelle was holding bobbed its head hard up and down and hit the sand over and over with one front foot. It looked mad. My queasiness returned with a vengeance.

"Hi, Ellen," said Michelle. "Belle's all ready." She held out a double-wide belt with handle-sized loops at the back and sides. Ellen stiff-legged over, leaned on her crutches and buckled the belt over her sweatshirt. The other riders already had on similar belts. This must be what I'm supposed to grab in case of emergency — if I wasn't running for my life.

A tan Accord drove in. And there he was, a short, steel post of a kid with hair buzzed off to hide the rubbed-out spots. "FRANKIE! FRANKIE! FRANKIE!" Sharp, insistent and too loud.

Mary shouted, "Hi, Joey! I ride Fur today."

Tim gave me a sympathetic smile. "Good luck," he whispered.

I sighed. Joey was the least of my worries.

Joey's father, a nearly bald man with a marathoner's build, caught up to his son. "We really appreciate you doing this, Frankie."

"I *really* like horses," Joey said enthusiastically. "Do you like horses, too, Frankie?"

I answered honestly, "Not as much as you do."

"Yeah," said Joey, "I *really* like horses."

"So why didn't you get on one last week?" I asked bluntly. Instead of making me come out here.

Air leaked from Joey. He rocked just a bit.

Get your wheels on the ground, Frankie! Don't take this out on the kid. This could be really good for him. I thought hard and said, "Okay, look ... you sit on the carpet, right? That's sort of furry ... like a horse. And Pookey's furry. You love to pat Pookey."

Joey nodded.

"And you sit in the car ... and the car moves. So ... a horse is ... a car-sized Pookey."

Joey lit up. "I *really* like horses. Will you help me?"

I shrugged. "That's why I'm here."

Joey pointed to Prince. "I want to ride that one."

Mary said smugly, "*He* ride Prince. *I* ride Fur."

Susan told Joey, "I'm not positive how Prince will react if you make a lot of noise. You know how you make a lot of noise sometimes. I think you should ride Fleur. She has more experience."

Joey started to rock again. His right hand waved in little circles. Oh-oh. Here it comes, I thought.

Then Maura-Lee said, "Prince ignores shouting when it's not directed at him."

"But I'll have to evaluate that first," said Susan.

"I'd trust Maura-Lee on this," Vanessa said. "Prince is quite bombproof."

Susan did not look pleased but said, "Okay, we'll try. But any hint of trouble and we stop immediately. The girls will get on their horses first to remind Joey how it's done."

"Come on, Mary," said Vanessa. "You're riding Fleur."

"I know," said Mary, smiling from ear to ear. She went over to a collection of short whips on a little ledge by the bleachers and picked one up. "I need this."

"No, I don't think so," Vanessa insisted gently. "You didn't need it last week, did you?"

"No," said Mary and she put the whip back and pointed to me. "Are his pants going to fall down?"

Vanessa smiled. "I hope not."

Mary asked me, "You have a girlfriend?"

"Now, Mary, you are here to ride," said Mary's mother. "You can visit with Frankie later."

"Okay," said Mary happily. "He can't be my boyfriend. Tim's my boyfriend."

Tim nodded, "I'm your Monday night boyfriend, all right." He guided Mary to the yellow-brown horse Kim held. Tim steadied the stirrup as Mary grunted and stretched, clinging to the saddle and Tim for balance, and shoved her left foot in place. Then Tim put a hand on Mary's shoulder and one behind her thigh and hefted her up onto the saddle. Kim got on the other side of the horse by Mary's knee, and Vanessa held Fleur's bridle.

"Okay, Mary," said Vanessa. "When you're ready, you tell her to go with a gentle little kick."

"Hi, Mom," called Mary, waving to her mother who stood outside the arena door. "Horses make Mom sneeze. She feels real icky," Mary announced as she rode Fleur down one side of the arena.

The other girl, Charlotte, mounted Strawberry, the rust-red pony. Then Patsy led the way with Charlotte's mother and Margaret as siderunners.

Ellen's horse, Belle — the second yellow-brown one — politely stepped sideways until she was parked next to a ramp. She stood statue still as Ellen swung herself aboard with Lana and Michelle's assistance. The girls then unstrapped Ellen's braces and placed her feet in the stirrups.

As each horse walked slow and steady, I had to admire their calmness. I might survive the evening after all.

"Your turn," Susan said to Joey. "You saw how the others got on. Do you think you can do that?"

Joey nodded. He held his arms up and his father carefully buckled the wide belt around him. Maura-Lee led Prince closer. His thick legs took scuffing steps in the sand. Sunlight streaming in the big doors bounced brown highlights off his dark fur. With his fat pink tongue leaking out the right corner of his mouth, he suddenly looked much more goofy than scary.

"Up you get, then," said Susan. She motioned to Joey.

Joey started rocking. His father frowned and looked expectantly at me. So did Susan. For that matter, so did Joey. Looking and waiting.

For what? It was up to him to get on the horse. I couldn't do it for him!

I said, "Remember, a horse is just a car-sized Pookey."

Joey nodded and said, "You first."

"What?"

"You first."

Me? My throat clamped shut. Me on a horse? No way! Joey just rocked ... and waited.

Susan passed me a riding helmet. I had no choice.

Sweat soaked my pits.

Yoga breaths. Yoga breaths. Don't let them see fear. Don't clench your jaw. Concentrate. Move carefully. Look cool. Be cool. I walked up to Prince. Prince yawned. His huge, black-lined teeth slanted forward — horror-movie teeth, big enough to rip my face off.

I tried to swallow. I couldn't. I ordered my feet to move. Left foot. Right foot. Left foot. I lifted my right foot and placed it in the stirrup.

"Other foot," said Maura-Lee.

For a few seconds mind-numbing embarrassment drowned my fear. I pretended to smile, and put my *left* foot in the stirrup. I pulled myself up by the saddle and swung my right leg over.

And there I was. On top of a horse. On top of a mountain of muscle with a mind of its own. And no one — not one person — saw the total terror inside me. It was the performance of a lifetime. I should add "actor" to my minuscule list of potential careers.

I fished for the opposite stirrup with my right foot. My darn toe wouldn't twist inward enough. Maura-Lee ducked under her horse's neck and took hold of my right ankle. She pushed the stirrup over my toe and looked at me with those body-piercing eyes. Then she smiled a very friendly smile and said in a voice that traveled no farther than my ears, "You could win an Oscar for this."

CHAPTER 9

Still Alive

I can tell you that Prince moved. I can tell you that I didn't get killed. I remember the saddle under my seat bones, the horse-heat on my calves, my heart pounding. But the questions shouting in my brain blotted out the rest: How did Maura-Lee know I was acting? How did Maura-Lee know I was afraid?

I knew I didn't give myself away. If I had, someone would have said "Don't worry" or "Prince is safe." No one did. No one said a thing.

There was only one explanation. The stories about Maura-Lee were true. *She read my mind!*

No, I was *losing* my mind. No one can read minds. *Or dream the future.*

But I *did* dream the petrel. I *did.* And if I could dream the future ...

Prince came to a halt in the streak of sunlight where we had started. "Okay, Joey. Your turn," said Susan. Her volume smacked me to attention. I looked at Joey. I truly hoped riding would be good for him and that he could do it by himself, because after that evening he was doing it without me. I was never, ever, going near Weird Maura-Lee again.

I dismounted, John Wayne smooth. I deserved that Oscar, all right. Joey beamed at me. "My turn, my turn," he said, and mounted without anyone's assistance. Susan tied a big knot in the reins and hung them on the horse's neck.

"Okay," said Susan. "You can make him go with a little bump of your heels."

Joey just smiled and waved his hands in the air, so Maura-Lee said "Walk on" to Prince and we walked on, Joey's father on the right, me on the left, directly behind Maura-Lee. Too close.

We walked and walked. I didn't think about getting stomped or bitten or squashed. Not once. True to my talentless nature, I only had the ability to freak about *one* thing at time. Horses were out; Weird Maura-Lee was in.

Was she reading my mind right now?

Susan gave loud, clear directions and even louder compliments for nearly an hour. I concentrated on my siderunner job, which actually got pretty boring. We stopped and stood for ages while Joey and the other riders (okay, mostly the other riders) did exercises. They circled their arms in the air, reached over and touched the top of the horse's head or rump. Stuff like that. There was never a need to hold Joey's belt loop or his knee.

A few times Prince turned his head, his thick fuzzy black ears pointed at me as if to say "This isn't so bad, is it?" His eyes were crinkled at the corners like someone who smiled a lot. I tried not to look at him. His head was too close to Maura-Lee. (And when he lifted his tail and plop, plop, plopped, his back end was too close, too.)

Mary talked the whole time, but Kim's quietness and Tim's tact kept her following Susan's directions fairly well. No one said anything to me. Hooves thumped. Saddles squeaked. The scents of damp sand, warm horse and fresh manure filled every breath. Strange — that part wasn't so bad.

At one point Joey made a breakthrough of sorts — he picked up the knot of reins in one hand. His normal stiffness softened into the movement of the horse's back. So *that* was the therapeutic part of therapeutic riding! It was hard not to enjoy the look of total happiness on his face.

Actually, everyone was grinning like crazy except me. And Maura-Lee. She had this intense look like Graham had the time he tried to skateboard with a sprained ankle. I wondered how many minds she was reading.

Finally Susan bellowed, "Well, that's it for tonight. Joey, you did GREAT!"

Joey's grin reached both ears. "I did great," he said. "I did great."

I had to hold Joey's belt loop as he dismounted, then we backed away from Prince and Maura-Lee. My job was done. Everyone paraded back to the barn. I stood outside the barn door with Joey and his father. I kept trying to catch Susan's eye, hoping to speed her to her car (and me to my home).

Two horses stuck their heads out of stalls as the gang came in: Kim's huge black monster and a black-and-white spotted one that pinned its ears flat as Michelle passed by. Michelle stomped her foot and the horse retreated. Saddles and bridles and neck straps were unbuckled and taken to a room at the far end of the barn and traded for small plastic bins full of brushes. Mary and Charlotte eagerly brushed Fleur and Strawberry, though Charlotte spent most of the time hugging Strawberry's neck. Ellen used Belle for support as she scruffed circles in the yellow-brown fur with a stiff plastic brush, then smoothed in a shine with a softer brush.

Joey's father said, "We have to go. Thank you very much, Frankie. You've been a godsend."

"It was nothing."

"I did great. I did great," Joey repeated for the tenth time.

"Yes, you did. You can ride a horse now."

"See you next time," Joey's father said, as he led his son to the car.

"Yeah, see ya," I lied.

Vanessa called to Maura-Lee, "It's your turn to do the manure. There's a new apple-picker by the back door. When's your ride coming?"

"Not till nine," Maura-Lee replied. "I have lots of time."

"If you want a drive home earlier, I'll ask my mom to wait for you," said Lana. "You live in town?"

"My dad's coming," said Maura-Lee.

"We're going to town. You could save him a trip," Lana insisted.

"I don't live in town." Maura-Lee's tone slammed the door on the subject.

The remaining riders all said thank-yous and good-nights (Mary said at least fifty) and left. Maura-Lee turned Prince out. Patsy led Strawberry toward the back door. As she passed the black-and-white horse, it struck its stall door with a big bang.

"No, Star, you're not getting out now. You and I are going for a ride." Patsy returned and led the spotted horse into the aisle. As Maura-Lee came by, Star flicked out his nose and bit the air next to Maura-Lee's ear!

"BACK OFF!" Maura-Lee barked.

"Don't shout at my horse!" Patsy snapped.

"He tried to bite me!"

"Star would never bite."

"You don't know how nasty your horse is."

"I *know* my horse!" Patsy was almost shouting. "I've been around horses since I was four years old. *You* only started *four* months ago. You read some *natural* garbage and you think you know everything!"

"I know he bites!"

Margaret jumped in. "At least he's not as bad as Tim's Jelly Bean." She laughed, obviously trying to cool things down.

"That's for sure," said Lana. "One day she's perfectly sweet and the next she'll take a piece out of you just for touching her!"

"I'll admit she *is* a little unpredictable," Tim agreed.

Lana laughed. "They say the only thing predictable about a mare is her unpredictability."

"Star is nothing like Jelly Bean," said Patsy sullenly. "Maura-Lee doesn't know what she's talking about."

"He tried to bite me!"

"HE DID NOT!"

"Girls!" Vanessa's voice rang through the barn. "How about you agree to disagree and leave it at that." It wasn't a question. It was an order.

Even from where I stood I swear I heard Maura-Lee's teeth grind. She grabbed the apple-picker, a many-toothed fork/shovel thing, and disappeared into the pasture.

I wandered to the rainbow fence to wait for Susan. The wind had softened, and layers of tan and rose clouds said that a spectacular sunset was in the works. I watched Prince walk slowly up behind the house, fold at the knees and drop into the damp grass. He rolled on his back, wiggling and grunting and flipping from side to side. Then he hoisted himself up, popped his butt in the air with a big squeal and trotted into the spruce forest at the top of the hill.

I smiled. Silly horse.

A burgundy Freestar van took away Lana, Margaret, Michelle and Kim.

Tim walked over. "You did good tonight."

"Yeah."

We waited in silence, watching the sky colors deepen, till Susan finally showed. "There you are, Frankie. Tim, want a lift?"

"No, thanks," said Tim. "I'm going to take The Ghost out for a spin."

I survived the drive home even though Susan talked almost as much as Mary. I stuck with Dad's rule, "just smile and nod." As we pulled to a stop in front of my house, Susan said, "I can't thank you enough for volunteering. See you Wednesday."

"Wednesday?"

"Didn't your dad explain? We meet twice a week, Mondays and Wednesdays, for ten weeks. This is week two."

I did the math. Seventeen more evenings with Maura-Lee? *Not* going to happen. I didn't know what to say, so I smiled and nodded.

I snuck in the back door. The smell of fish chowder jumped me. Ugh. I walked quietly down to my room, in no mood to talk. Thankfully, Dad was asleep in front of the TV and Mom was busy on her laptop. I didn't worry about Bernie — she always ignored me. I closed my bedroom door and flopped on my bed in a black mood and —

The petrel! I'd actually forgotten the petrel! The poor thing was trapped in a cardboard box, scared and starving, and I had forgotten it!

I rushed to my closet and carefully peeked into the box. Was it dead? I ticked the cardboard with my fingernail.

One wing stirred. Layers of dark feathers on the tiny head closed tighter. I sighed all the way down to my socks.

"Hi, little fella."

I took out the hot water bottle. An eye opened. The bird shifted its weight and tried to stand, but up was still sideways and it rolled on its side. Its feathers were dry now. And not black at all, but actually a dark sooty brown.

The newspapers were damp. Had it bumped the bowl or actually been drinking? If it was drinking on its own, all I had to do was get food into it and it would be as right as rain in no time!

What did petrels eat?

I Googled "petrel." 5,937,000 hits. I tried again. "Petrel" ... "bird" ... "Nova Scotia." Bingo. A Wilson's Storm-petrel. *Oceanites oceanicus.* Or maybe a Leach's Storm-petrel. They were only seen over the ocean. All the descriptions were for birds in flight, not huddled in a box. I read more. *The characteristic yellow webbing between the toes of the Wilson's Storm-petrel is almost never observed without having the bird in hand.* I went over and carefully spread the tiny warm toes, like itty-bitty duck feet. Yellow webs. A Wilson's for sure.

I surfed for more info. *Primitive birds. Tubular nostrils for excreting excess salt.* So that's what that extra little beak thing was. Strange. *Spend most of their lives at sea. Visit land only to breed. Lay eggs in burrows in the ground.* Cool! I never heard of birds living underground! *Breed in the southern hemisphere as far south as Antarctica. Migrate to the North Atlantic as far as Labrador for summer.* Wow, that's far! *Feed by hovering just above the surface of the water, picking up small crustaceans, squid, fish ... follow ships and whales ... attracted by the leftovers.*

I looked up "crustaceans." Shrimp, krill, crabs, lobsters. Mom had canned lobster in the cupboard. And then there was her disgusting fish chowder. I hurried to the kitchen and spooned some white flakes of fish from the chowder, even though I'd rather stand over a steaming pile of horse manure.

Back in my room, I waved a thumbnail-sized bite in front of the petrel. No reaction. "Mmm, yummy," I pretended. I rubbed it across the bird's tube-shaped nostrils. Still no reaction. "Okay, you asked for it." As gently as possible, I pried opened its beak and placed the fish on its pointy pink tongue.

The petrel exploded to life. It rose up, shaking its head violently. The fish vanished over my shoulder and the bird rolled upside down.

I righted the petrel and tried again. It fought my effort to pry apart its beak, but I got it open and pushed the next bit of fish down the bird's throat. In an instant the fish hit me in the face. "Gross!" My last effort ended with fish in my hair.

"Why won't you eat?" I racked my brain. Then it occurred to me that fish from the chowder might taste more like onions or milk.

I fetched a can of lobster and tried that. I never did find the two pieces that rocketed into my closet.

"I'm supposed to save you, little bird. How can I do that if you won't eat?" I forced back tears. Then went to the bathroom to wash. My fingers stank. My face stank. My hair stank. Three soapings later I still smelled fishy.

I got back on the computer. Not one word about how to feed an injured petrel. Then I thought of how I had thrown up for almost twenty-four hours after my concussion. So maybe it was too soon. The bird would eat tomorrow.

Or not. Maybe Mom was right. *Let nature take its course.* Why couldn't I ever learn? As if *I* could ever fix a bird! What did *I* know?

Suddenly a thought grabbed me. "Nothing!" I answered myself and smiled. "But Cannon knows tons!"

Cannon often talked about birds. He'd tell his classes all about the latest local sightings — where the bird came from, how rare it was in case anyone wanted to check it off their life list. Cannon had a life list of birds a mile long. He had more sightings than anyone in Nova Scotia. He knew all about birds. He loved birds.

I wondered if Cannon had ever seen a Wilson's Storm-petrel up close. I bet he'd like to. And I bet he knew what to do for it!

I happily surfed the net for a while — found a cool new skateboard site, looked up "hippotherapy" (no hippos, just horses) and then got ready for bed. Tomorrow would be a simple ollie and grind day. I had two clear goals.

One, ask Cannon about the petrel.

Two, avoid Maura-Lee.

CHAPTER 10

Weird Maura-Lee

My night filled with endless dreams — late for school, late for a test, studied the wrong chapter, broke my skateboard, lost my lunch money.

I woke up with a sore jaw and rawness inside my cheeks. The first thing I did was check the petrel. Its tiny eyes peered at me with a crooked stare. "Hi, little fellow," I whispered. "You're sitting up straighter today! That's great. You get some more rest and I'll get you some food. My science teacher is going to help with that. You're going to be fine. See you later."

As I opened my door a brown-and-black fur-ball streaked for my room. "Oh, no you don't!" I caught Pookey with the side of my foot and punted her into a claw-screeching skid along the hardwood hallway. She must have smelled the bird. Or the lost bits of fish. *I* could still smell the fish. I closed my door tightly.

I was buried in a big bowl of cereal and raisins when Dad came into the kitchen. "How'd it go last night?" he asked.

The truth would invite a major "I told you so," so I mmphed through a mouthful, like I'd answer when I could.

Mom came in. She had on a soft orange blouse that went well with her leftover tan — definitely her color. "This is going to be a great day!"

"How do you know?" Dad asked, giving her a hug.

"I feel it in my gut," said Mom, squeezing him back. Then she belched noisily in Dad's ear. "Guess it was just gas." She laughed and pulled away.

"Come back here, you!"

"Oh-oh, the Scronker!" Mom gasped.

Dad rubbed Mom's back with his big hands. "How about the Massager instead?"

Mom sagged in his arms and moaned. "I think you should call that one the Melter. If I could bottle and sell your hugs, we'd be rich!"

"We've got the Melter, the Massager, the Smug, the Scronker, the Snuggy-huggy —"

"Don't forget the Monkey." Mom hopped up and wrapped both legs around Dad's. "And everyone's favorites — the Bear Hug and the Cheek-to-Cheek."

"And *my* favorite — the Groper!"

"Bob!"

"We'll sell a variety pack, too. For those who can't make up their minds."

"You mean for men," Mom teased. "Frankie, you want a hug?"

"NO!" I reserved hugs for birthdays and being rescued from tigers.

"Hugs are good medicine."

"The Medicine Hug!" said Dad. "Bottle that one for sure. Sell it by prescription only."

Bernie came in. "Get a room, you two. Pee-yew, it smells like a barn in here."

That would be my sneakers. I gulped down the last bite and bolted out the door before Dad remembered his unanswered question. I hummed down the sidewalk. The bearings on my skateboard hummed with me, though more out of tune. They weren't drying well with all the damp weather, and Mom stopped letting me use her hairdryer after the night I left it on and nearly barbecued the garage.

But Mom was right about the day. Everything was clear. The sidewalks, the sky, my goals. First — Cannon. I had him for second period, just before recess. Second — Maura-Lee. In order to avoid her I had to know where she was without being obvious. No problem. I'd been invisible for years.

The wind tasted like fall. It helped speed me down Elm Street and halfway up the next hill. If it wasn't for the three-way stop, I'd have had enough speed on the last hill to roll right through the school's big front doors.

When I walked into homeroom, I glanced at the back wall, pretending to read the anti-bullying posters while locating Maura-Lee. Her assigned seat in the center of the room was occupied, but I had to look twice to confirm it was her. Blond and burgundy streaked her brown ponytail. Bangs of each color fell over her eyes.

I skirted around the room and took my seat in the back corner. This year I had Roddie beside me, and the Melanson twins, Leon and Leonard, on the other side of him, leaving me to make the last row look smart. The Melanson twins were of one mind but could never decide which one was using it. And though I suspected Roddie was smart, his mind wandered so far and so fast, bloodhounds couldn't track it. But he always said "miss" and "sir," and smiled and shook hands, so he practically got away with murder. Not that Roddie would hurt a soul … except himself. He was the reason helmets and knee pads were invented.

Lana and Patsy wandered in. They both smiled straight at me and waved. I thought Roddie was going to lose it. "When did *those* girls start noticing skater dude?" he blurted.

"Get a board," I said. "Chicks dig boards."

Lana sat down and Patsy headed for her seat next to Maura-Lee, but she suddenly stiffened and threw Maura-Lee a look that dropped the temperature of the room by ten degrees. What was that about?

Mrs. Rose, our homeroom and history teacher, leaned against her desk, smiling her crooked smile, the big lump on the side of her nose pushing her glasses off to one side. She was as tough as she was good-looking, but no one gave her a hard time because she loved history (which made the class bearable) and loved kids (unlike some teachers), and that meant the kids loved her. She talked for a bit and then said, "Okay, let's hear your assignments. Who'd like to read first?"

Half the class raised their hands. Reading out loud earned extra points. And some kids could really write — another talent I lacked. I didn't put up my hand. As each person went to the front of the room and read their two or three pages, the rest listened or doodled or passed notes or text messaged or dozed off. Mrs. Rose knocked people to attention now and then by asking questions. I was in the middle of my eighth rehearsal of what I was going to say to Cannon when Mrs. Rose exclaimed, "Roddie! What on earth are you doing?"

Roddie had his T-shirt pulled up under his chin and was drawing circles around his nipples with a red marker. It was one of Mrs. Rose's white-board markers, the kind that washed right off, but I snatched it from Roddie and pretended to read the label.

"Waterproof. Indelible. Permanent."

Mrs. Rose never cracked a wrinkle. In a perfectly calm, consoling tone, she said, "Roddie, you're going to look pretty funny on the beach next summer."

The look on Roddie's face was worth a fully pimped Civic! The class nearly rolled out the doors laughing. Mrs. Rose finally got control and asked Patsy to read her assignment, which was actually interesting. Then Mrs. Rose asked, "Lana, would you like to go next?"

Maura-Lee thrust up her hand. "I will, Miss."

Patsy glared at Maura-Lee again, and the temperature dropped to near freezing. Lana fumbled with her scribbler, but Maura-Lee jumped up, marched to the blackboard and faced the class.

That's when I understood. Maura-Lee was dressed exactly like Patsy. Except Maura-Lee had long sleeves and Patsy's were short. Maura-Lee had on the same colors in the same style — right down to the lacey bits around the neck and the trim on the hem of her jeans! And her hair and makeup screamed "mirror image." It was freaking amazing.

As she read, she tilted her head exactly the way Patsy did. And held her paper and played with her dangling earrings ... just like Patsy! *All* the girls looked at Patsy — some with sympathy, most like NASCAR spectators eager for a car crash.

By the time Maura-Lee had finished reading and sauntered to her desk, I knew four things. One: Maura-Lee was breaking the number-one girls' rule on purpose. Two: her perfect imitation was the most brilliant passive-aggressive behavior I had ever seen! Three: Maura-Lee was really pretty. And four: there was only one way Maura-Lee knew what Patsy was going to wear.

The buzzer sounded. I bolted for the hall. No time to think about weird stuff. Cannon's class was next.

But I couldn't help it. There was the day Mary Alice screamed ... and the day Maura-Lee wore all preppy — just like Leanne ... and the day she wore soft peach frills and a super curly do — a perfect Kaitlin clone. God help anyone who ticked off Maura-Lee.

One more reason to avoid her.

In Cannon's classroom I took a back corner seat again, as far from the drama as I could get. Cannon bounced in, striding off the balls of his feet like he was hiking uphill. He smiled in his usual are-you-going-to-love-what-I-have-to-teach-you-today way and announced that the forecast looked good for Wednesday. Blastoff was scheduled for the second period.

For the next forty minutes I concentrated and took careful notes. When the recess buzzer rang, I stayed put until Cannon finished feeding papers into his worn briefcase. Then I kept pace with him down the hall.

I cleared my throat. "Um, um. Sir?"

"Uccello. What can I do for you?"

That's another thing the kids liked about him. He knew everyone's name by the end of the first week in September. My heart raced.

"I, ah, I found this injured Wilson's Storm-petrel. If I could figure out what to feed it, I think it'd be all right. I thought you could tell me what to do."

Mr. Cannon paused. He looked at me for a moment and said, "Kill it."

CHAPTER 11

Fish

I tried to swallow. Cannon was kidding, right? Of course he was kidding. He was famous for his sense of humor. Any moment he was going to wink and say, "Got you, Frankie!"

Instead he said, "Petrels are plankton eaters. You can't go sieve the ocean for plankton. Put it down."

"Petrels eat fish, too, right?"

Cannon's face softened. He looked over his glasses. "If you can't do it yourself, bring it to me. I'll put it out of its misery."

And he left me standing alone in a hallway full of conversations and laughter. I don't know how long I stood there wanting to run after him, wanting to shake my fists in his face and swear enough to turn his pathetic comb-over white. Finally, I just went to my locker, got my gear and walked out. I didn't care if anyone stopped me. Actually, I wished someone would try. Just try to stop me. Go ahead and try.

No one saw me leave school.

I took the long way home. I couldn't face the petrel. The wind had warmed and strong gusts pushed me along. As I turned onto Hawthorne Street I smelled the garbage truck before I saw it. I suddenly hated the garbage man. Him and his half a face and ugly dog. It was all his fault. Those stories about him were probably true.

The big brown truck slowed. I kicked up my board and moved off the sidewalk to let a mom with a double baby buggy and a panting Chow Chow go past.

Tires gritted against the curb. "How's the petrel doing?"

I refused to look at him. "It won't eat." I got back on my board. End of conversation.

He didn't take the hint. The truck rolled along at my speed. "What have you tried?"

"Fish."

"What type of fish?"

Are you totally blind? I don't want to talk to you! I took a breath and nearly choked on blue-gray exhaust. "Haddock and lobster."

"Hmm, I should be so lucky. Fresh?"

"Mom wouldn't cook fish that wasn't fresh. And I just opened the can of lobster last night."

"I'm sorry," he said. "I meant fresh as in raw. Canned foods are cooked. Maybe the bird didn't know what to do with cooked food."

It knew what to do — spit it in my face. Still, I hadn't thought about cooked versus raw. I felt as dim as Alaska in December. But the relief in my gut told me he was right. I looked up past the huge drooling dog into the man's one good eye. He said, "Give it a try, eh?" and drove away.

I headed back the way I'd come, up past the school, across the Trans-Canada at the traffic lights and over to the four big box stores where the forest was two years ago. Downtown Killers, Mom called them.

At the fish counter I found ten kinds of raw fillets. I pointed to the North Atlantic perch. That sounded right.

"What's the freshest?" I asked.

"It's all fresh. It came in on Monday."

"But Monday was yesterday. And when was it caught?"

The clerk just shrugged. "You want some or not?"

I bet he wasn't rude to his adult customers. "I'll take one piece."

He sealed it in a small plastic bag, weighed, labeled and put it in another plastic bag with handles. At the checkout the cashier dropped it into a third plastic bag, with the store's logo on the sides. I poked the package into my backpack, annoyed that I could still smell the fish through the three layers of plastic.

No one home except Pookey and the petrel. I put on a pair of rubber gloves from under the sink and chopped the fish into beak-sized slivers. Pookey leaned along my legs and yowled. I tossed a fat chunk into her bowl to keep her from chasing me to my room, put the rest in a plastic container and hid it behind the warehouse of containers already choking the refrigerator so Mom wouldn't find it.

The petrel's head still slanted a little to one side, but it sat in the middle of the box, upright, not leaning on anything. Excellent!

"I found you some *fresh* fish, little fellow. It's from the Atlantic Ocean, just like you are. Mmmm, yummy."

I carefully stuck my fingernail between the upper and lower bills, opened them and laid a strip of fish on the darting tongue. The bird closed its eyes for a moment and stretched its neck up. Then flick, out went the fish and over went the petrel.

My stomach churned. I sat the bird upright and tried again. And again. "Bird, you *have* to eat!" My throat hurt. "Please, little bird. I got this fish especially for you. All you have to do is swallow." No go.

"Okay, bird, if you die, it's not my fault."

I stood up and closed the closet door. I felt like slamming it. I fell on my bed. I could still smell fish. My backpack stank. The fish bag had leaked onto a yellow handout. I carefully picked up one dry corner and headed for the kitchen garbage. The name "Pascarelli" caught my eye. Sounded Italian. Not many Italian names around besides ours. I unfolded the paper.

Career Exploration ... V.I. Pascarelli ... Biologist ... ninth grade assembly ... Tuesday afternoon.

Tuesday. Today.

I had to get back to school! Kids always tried to sneak out of assemblies. Mrs. Rose would be counting heads. If I didn't make it, I'd get detention for a week! All because of some soon-to-be-dead bird.

As I burned back to school, a thought wiggled up, a tiny worm of hope. If V.I. Pascarelli was a biologist, maybe he could tell me more about feeding a petrel.

The second lunch buzzer went off just as I rolled into the schoolyard. Tim caught me in the cafeteria and punched me hard on the shoulder. "Where were you, man? I looked for you at recess. I must have been going up one flight of stairs when you were going down the other. Like, fifty times. I can't believe I never found you."

"Yeah, funny thing." Tim had been with me the day the last little bird died. If I told him about the petrel, he'd lecture me just like Mom.

Mike showed up and filled the next half hour with words. All I had to do was sit there and try not to think about the petrel and my one last chance. I didn't succeed.

The loud speaker reminded the ninth graders to go to the audio-visual room when the bell rang. Bored of the cafeteria, Tim and Mike and I wandered over early, but we weren't the first ones there. Five chatty girls surrounded someone in the end seat next to the stage. Must be Pascarelli. No chance for me to ask my question, but at least that meant he was approachable.

The guys and I sat in the back row. The librarian, Mrs. Delorey, stepped up on stage and tested the microphone. The huddle of girls took front-row seats, letting me see the center of their attention. So much for luck. It was just Vanessa. She must be interested in biology, too.

"Good afternoon," said Mrs. Delorey. The mike squealed. "Oh, dear." She blushed, fiddled with some buttons and then continued. "Today I'm sure you'll appreciate meeting our first speaker in the new Career Exploration Series." She began to read from a paper, "V.I. Pascarelli has a masters degree in biology from the University of Toronto and is currently working as a research technician studying the osmotic regulation of Fun ... Fun-du-lus heter ... heter-oc ..." She lowered the paper. "Why don't I let her take it from here?"

Her?

Vanessa climbed the three steps to the stage. She didn't use the microphone. In her clear, round voice she said, "Good afternoon. I'm Vanessa Isabelle Pascarelli, but that doesn't usually fit in the spaces provided, so I started going by V.I. Pascarelli. What Mrs. Delorey was trying to say was Fundulus heteroclitis, commonly called killifish. Around here they're known as mum-michogs. They're an amazing little fish. They can live in salt water and fresh water and in extreme temperatures and high levels of pollution. They were the very first fish in outer space, part of an experiment on the Skylab in 1973."

"You never said Vanessa was a biologist," I whispered to Tim.

He shrugged. "You never asked."

Vanessa talked about why she got into biology and how she ended up at the university in Antigonish. She told some hilarious stories about getting stuck in the muck while catching mummichogs, and some pretty neat stuff about how their gills were helping to find a cure for cystic fibrosis. She was really good. The audience laughed and asked questions and gave her humongous applause when she was done.

As the room emptied, the Hug a Horse Farm gang closed in on Vanessa. I waited till the buzzer sounded and they headed for their classes. Maura-Lee stepped up, said something to Vanessa, then walked away slowly, tucking the burgundy curls behind her ears. I moved in.

"Hi, Frankie," said Vanessa.

"Do you know what I could feed a Wilson's Storm-petrel?" I asked quietly. "It hit its head, but it's going to be okay if I can get it to eat."

Vanessa looked thoughtful. "Hmmm, that's a tough one. I'd guess fresh fish would work."

I couldn't hide my disappointment. "I tried that."

"Mind you, it's hard to get really fresh fish from the grocery stores. Here we are, right next to the ocean, and all the store fish comes from the other end of the province, or New Brunswick, or even Quebec! Those big chain stores, they'll be the death of small towns like ours. Sorry, I digress. I'm good at that."

Mom would like Vanessa.

"I suppose the best thing to do," she said, "is to go fishing yourself."

Mrs. Delorey walked over and gave me a stern get-to-class look.

"Good luck," said Vanessa.

Fishing. It'd been years since Dad and I went fishing together. He could stand for hours over a pool waiting for a trout to taste his worm. I found it mind-numbing. Usually I'd just stretch out in the grass and watch the clouds while Dad obsessed over every ripple.

After school the wind died and the sun pushed away the cool air. Dad was in the garage gassing up the rototiller.

"Nice afternoon for fishing."

"Fishing?"

"Yeah, you want to go?"

He suddenly got all puppy-waiting-for-a-ball eager. "Great idea! I'd love to wet my line in a nice quiet pool." But then he heaved his wide shoulders and sighed. "Too much to do. I have to get the lawn mowed and that bed out back tilled so your mother can plant all those bulbs I made the mistake of buying. So, why the sudden interest in fishing?"

"I just thought ... ah ..." I ground gears working out an excuse. "I just thought that Mom might like some *fresh* fish after that stinky stuff she cooked last night."

"That's a nice thought, but this time of year it's only catch and release."

"Oh." So that was that. No fishing. There was nothing more I could do. The petrel was doomed. Mom was right. I never learn.

I made a decision. I wasn't going to watch it starve to death. After supper I would take it down to the Landing, where the rivers met the salt water and long-leggy birds and ducks lived nearly year round. I would place the petrel in the tall grass and leave. It would live or it would die. Nature would take its course.

"Are you okay?" Dad asked. "You don't look good."

"I'm fine."

"Good. Then you can mow while I till."

I didn't mind mowing.

"Now, mow east and west," he instructed, "and point the cuttings away from the flower beds."

"I know, I know."

"If you start by the back step and go along —"

"Dad! It's just grass!"

"On second thought, I'll do it."

I rolled my eyes and sighed. "You have *got* to get a life!"

"It has to be done right!"

"I promise." He didn't trust me with his precious lawn. Last June I wrote my initial in fertilizer across our rather large backyard. A week later, a giant dark green F pushed up past the rest of the lighter green lawn. It was cool! But Dad didn't think so. I've never seen his face that shade of red. After several new combinations of unpleasant words, he pointed out that I may know it was just my initial but it was also the first letter of a very different word. What would the neighbors think? He carefully fertilized the rest of the lawn to erase my bright idea, but the F didn't completely disappear until late August.

I pushed the mower around back, pulled the engine to life and headed due east. Small gas engines ruled the rest of the afternoon. Then Mom made one of my favorite suppers — pan-fried hamburger and twice-cooked potatoes. All that time I managed to keep my mind away from the box in my closet, but finally I ended up flopped on my bed, a bucket of *whys* sloshing around in my head.

Why did I have that dream? *Why* see the future if you couldn't do anything about it? *Why* did I pick up the bird? *Why* wouldn't it eat? *Why* couldn't I do anything right? *Why* did it hurt so much? Tears ran over my cheeks and into my ears. I rolled onto my stomach and soaked my pillow until I sank into a numb half-sleep.

The front door knocker sounded three sharp raps. Moments later Mom clicked her fingernails on my bedroom door and opened it. "There's someone at the door for you."

Someone? Mom knew everyone I knew. I rolled over. "Who is it?"

Mom smiled a silly smile. "A *girl*," she said, and sighed an exaggerated sigh. "It was bound to happen some time. She said she wouldn't come in, so hurry up. It's not polite to leave a guest on the doorstep."

I went to the front hall. Mom hovered in the kitchen, just out of sight. I opened the door.

It was Maura-Lee.

CHAPTER 12

Trout

Maura Lee thrust out a plastic sandwich box with one hand and pulled up the lid with the other. Light glinted off the silver scales of a trout as long as a slice of bread. "For the petrel," she said. "It's fresh." She snapped the lid back on and pushed the box at me. I had to take it. Then she spun around, strode down the front walk, picked up her bike and peddled away, burgundy, blonde and brown curls flying out behind.

"Why didn't you invite her in?" Mom's voice sounded right in my ear. I jumped. "She was ... I just forgot this at school."

"Oh," said Mom, a little suspicious and a lot disappointed. "Pretty girl. Do I know her?"

"It's just Maura-Lee."

"Maura-Lee Chisholm? Good grief! You kids grow up so fast it makes my head spin. She looks so different than she did in second grade."

Than she did yesterday, I thought.

"She ... she's a very smart girl. And she certainly is very pretty now," said Mom, making too obvious an effort to sound positive. "Are you two friends?"

"NO!"

"Oh," she said. Was that relief? "Hmm, she *was* an odd little kid. I suppose it's no wonder, after what happened."

I wanted to ask what happened and then again I didn't. Talking to my mom about a girl was gross. And when the girl was Maura-Lee, well ...

"But she *is* smart," Mom repeated, "*and* pretty. And her father *is* a very nice man."

What's her father got to do with anything? "Mom, she's *not* my friend!"

"Okay, dear." She didn't believe me.

I groaned and stomped to my room, more creeped out than annoyed. How did Maura-Lee know I needed fresh fish? The creepy feeling crawled between my shoulder blades. Then I remembered her walking away as I talked with Vanessa. Of course! She overheard me. Simple.

I dropped the sandwich box on my dresser. I had already decided about the petrel. But here was a trout. *Fresh* fish. Would the bird spit it out, too? Probably.

A splash and a *whack, whack* of wings striking cardboard made me jump. "Hang on. I'm coming." I hurried to the closet. The petrel stood up. "You're standing!" I exclaimed, at which its left foot curled under and the bird rolled on its side. "Oh, well. But you did *good*. Real good! And I've got honest-to-goodness *fresh* fish for you. You'll like it."

I rooted around my dresser and found my old pocket knife. I sawed through the icky slime. Tiny, iridescent scales clung to the knife and plastic box. I hacked off a bit of pale pink flesh. Totally not-smelly flesh. No smell at all!

"Okay, bird. This is it. Eat or die."

The petrel resisted opening its beak, twisting its head this way and that, and striking at my hands with its wings. Strong little wings. Then, for an instant it gave in. I forced open the beak and got the bit of trout in as far as its tongue. The bird thrust its bill forward, seized the fish and gulped it down!

My heart thudded. "Yes!" My hands trembled as I carved off another morsel.

Lunge. Gulp.

"Yes! Yes! Yes! Yes! Yes!" I couldn't smile wide enough. I filled the feathered appetite until its neck bulged and it lost all interest. Then I stroked the soft charcoal-brown feathers between its wings. "You're going to be fine. You're going to fly." My heart soared. I knew I was in big trouble. I would be completely crushed if the petrel didn't return to the air, but at that moment I flew on wings of joy.

Until a practical thought sucked me back to earth. The trout was half gone. There was only enough left for tomorrow morning. The bird needed at least one more day to recover. *I needed more fish.* I could sneak out Dad's fishing gear, figure out how to put the rod and reel together, string the line, tie the hook, dig bait, find a stream — one with fish in it, catch a fish and not get caught by the law. Or ... I could ask Maura-Lee where she got the trout.

My evening filled with grass to rake, homework to read and repeats on TV. I went to bed not one toenail closer to another trout. I fished all night long, dream after dream, and never caught a thing.

Sunlight pulled me awake. The petrel ate the remaining trout, except the backbone and head. It stood upright the whole time and only tottered a bit. A pile of black and white droppings in the corner of the box proved things were working well. All I needed was more trout.

I grabbed three oatmeal chocolate-chip cookies and an apple and ran out the back door before I heard all of Dad's lecture about healthy breakfasts and healthy minds. Bombing down the Elm Street hill, my head filled with wings, short round black wings. At the bottom, I leaned back, skidded to a stop. I knew what I had to do.

If those wings were going to fly I *had* to talk to Maura-Lee. Ask her where she got the trout, and if there might be another one. It was out of season, undersize and illegal, but I would ask.

At school, kids squealed, jostled and laughed almost like the day before Christmas vacation. Second period was Blastoff so the first-period teachers didn't stand a chance. Who could focus with such a major event about to explode?

Not me. But not because of Blastoff. Because of Maura-Lee. She seemed so calm. Her hair was all brown again and pulled up in two high wavy pigtails held with galloping-horse clips. She didn't have any makeup on, but she was still really pretty. Why hadn't I noticed that before?

I scanned the classroom for her latest victim. There were no matches. So was this the *real* Maura-Lee? The more I watched, the more normal she seemed. The idea that she could read minds became as absurd as me spreading my arms and flying. Boy, did I need to get my tires rotated. Maura-Lee had overheard the other girls talking about what they were going to wear, just like she overheard me talking to Vanessa. Girls talked about clothes all the time.

But how did she know I was afraid of horses? Same way. While everyone else yakked — she watched. I must have given her a clue. Had to be it. Simple.

When the buzzer rang, the class bolted. Maura-Lee took her time. I did, too. "So, where did you get the fish?"

"It's a trout," she said bluntly. "Did the petrel eat it?"

"Yeah."

"All of it?"

"Yeah."

"The next one should be bigger."

"Okay."

"I can't get it after school today. I'm taking the bus to Hug a Horse. Do you know how to kill a trout?"

"I, ah ... you mean *catch* a trout?"

"No."

I thought for a sec, then said, "Dad used to hit the fish over the head to knock it out and then cut off its head real quick. It looked gross but he said it was humane."

She nodded. "Then we can go fishing. Right now."

"We?"

"I hate killing fish."

"But we'll miss Blastoff!"

"Good." She looked me right in the eye. Hers were the color of unsweetened chocolate and slanted down at the corners. "The next chance is tomorrow evening. The bird has to eat before then."

"Yes, but ..."

"But what?"

I sighed and nodded. While all eyes were on Cannon in the soccer field out back, Maura-Lee and I walked out the front doors.

I followed her up Hawthorne Street and across Thorne Ridge with its new condos and rutted, dirt yards. Then down the steep path to the river, full enough to float a truck.

"Is this where you caught the fish?"

"Of course not."

"But how ...?"

"There's a U-fish pond up behind the dairy."

We kept near the river on a graveled trail, concrete hard from years of jogging feet and bicycles. Shattered tree trunks, the remains of long-dead elms, lined the route. Mom often talked about what the elm trees around town used to be like before Dutch elm disease wiped them out. Giant umbrellas of leaves, she said. The town was a lot cooler then.

"Sad how all the elm trees are gone," I said, trying to fill the silence.

"They're not *all* gone."

"Oh."

The river flowed smooth and silent, and the drone

of midtown traffic reached us on the still air. Maura-Lee's legs were as long as mine but she walked faster and I worked to keep up. We came to the giant Highland dancer, carved out of one of the dead elms. She was painted in gaudy blue-and-yellow tartan and looked awkward, with her neck and arms shaped from thick upward-pointing branches not quite at right angles. There were a bunch of these chainsaw sculptures around town, all made from dead trees: two old-time soldiers, a Scotsman with a huge claymore, a caber tosser, two curlers, a scowling priest and, my favorite, a grand piper who played silently (the only way bagpipes sound good).

The trail led through Cairn Park with its monuments built by local Scottish clans. Clan Chattan had erected a rough vertical slab of rock as tall as a man. I didn't know any Chattans in Antigonish, but there were tons of MacDonalds. Their cairn was shaped like a lighthouse with shiny black stone plaques on the sides, a crest and a name on each — Sleat, MacDonald, Clanranald, McDonnell of Glengarry ... I couldn't read the other sides from the path.

Rounded beach stones cemented together and decorated with patches of yellow-green lichen stood for the MacDougalls: *Dedicated July 1981 to the memory of our MacDougall forebears by the clan MacDougall Society of Antigonish to commemorate a worthy inheritance of high achievement and service to cod and country.* That's what it looked like it said — maybe their ancestors were fishermen.

The last one had all sizes of field stones in dirty brown mortar stacked in a column. The Chisholms.

"Did your family help build that?"

"No!"

"You're a Chisholm."

"There are sixty-four Chisholms in the phone book."

"Oh." Only one Uccello.

We walked in silence to the bridge. The sign at one end read "Wrights River." The one at the other end read "Rights River." Typical. We crossed just as a tandem dump truck barreled around the blind curve ahead, its jack-hammer engine brakes smashing the quiet. Maura-Lee put her hands over her ears, turned right and walked along the train tracks.

We followed the rails past the dairy and up a steep bank on a path the dirt-bikers hadn't found yet. At the top, Maura-Lee pushed through a clump of spruce trees. The path, thickly padded with years of brown needles, ended near a pond about the size of our school gymnasium.

The old mobile home perched on a hill beyond looked pretty beat up. Literally. Like someone had taken a hammer and pounded dents in the side.

"Boy, whoever lives here must have quite a temper."

Maura-Lee shot me a hard look. "What are you talking about?"

"The dents in the trailer."

She relaxed. "I think that was hail."

She went around the pond to a small red shed. A plastic-covered poster on one door read "Speckled

Trout = \$4.00 Rainbow Trout = \$8.00" in fat black marker. Maura-Lee ducked inside and came out with a dish filled with small, light brown pellets and a net with a handle as long as she was tall.

"What are you doing?"

"Getting you a trout."

"Shouldn't we ask?"

"There's no one home."

"We can't just steal it!"

"We're not stealing."

"What do you call sneaking in the back way and taking a fish without asking?"

"We weren't *sneaking in the back way*," she huffed. "It was just the *shortest* way. I'll pay for it later."

"Okay, okay. But I don't get it. What's to keep someone from fishing the pond dry?"

"No one would do that."

"Slug would."

Maura-Lee smirked. "No, he wouldn't." She obviously knew something I didn't.

"Why?"

She pointed to a rusty steel post holding a white wooden sign: BEWARE OF UGLY DOG!

"You never said anything about a *dog!*"

"Oh, for Pete's sake! The dog's not home, either."

"But the sign —"

"Works, doesn't it?"

She was right. It was the word *ugly* that got to me. Did it mean terrible to look at or nasty? I didn't want to find out. "What if the dog —"

"The dog's not home! Now, do you want the stupid fish or not?"

"You don't have to get your knickers in a knot!"

She looked at me blankly for a moment, then snorted, "Knickers in a knot. No one says *that* anymore."

"Nanna did."

"Did?"

"She died."

Maura-Lee nodded.

"So, how are we going to catch this fish without a fishing rod?"

"Just watch." She pulled a Swiss Army Knife from her jeans and opened a thin, sharp blade. Then she picked up a fist-sized rock and passed them both to me. "You have to kill it as soon as it hits the ground."

I shrugged. "Okay."

She went out on the deck that hung over the edge of the pond and sprinkled a few pellets from the dish onto the water's surface. *Schloop,* one disappeared. *Schloop. Blurp.* Two more gone. Suddenly, *splash, thrash,* the water boiled with shining trout fighting for the remaining food. Maura-Lee tossed in the rest of the pellets and plunged the net into the feeding frenzy. She yanked out the heaving net and slapped it on the deck. "Hit it quick!" she ordered.

A trout swam in the air, arching its deep pink sides and whacking its tail in panic. I dropped the knife and tried to hold the slimy, arm-thick body still, but it twisted out of my grasp.

"Now!" Maura-Lee panted.

I grabbed it again and brought the rock down hard. The trout shivered and was still. Maura-Lee kicked the knife closer.

"Quick," she begged. The fish jumped when the sharp blade bit through its spine. Maura-Lee flinched.

And there it lay, a magnificent, fat, pink-striped rainbow trout as long as my forearm. Maura-Lee returned the net and dish while I rinsed off the slime and blood.

Maura-Lee came back with a plastic bag, put her hand inside and grabbed the trout, inverting the bag over it so she didn't have to touch the fish. A rumble approached from beyond the trailer.

"Let's go," Maura-Lee ordered, and headed for the spruce trees.

"What if that's the owner? We can pay for the fish."

Maura-Lee spun around. "Do you have eight dollars on you?"

"I, ah, no ... but ..."

"I said I'll pay for it later." The vehicle rumbled closer. As I reached the first tree, I heard a massive *woof*.

"RUN!" Maura-Lee shouted. "And don't look back!"

Yeah, right. That was like telling a mountain climber, *don't look down*. I looked back and, in that nanosecond, I recognized the drooling, cinder-block head of the garbage man's dog barreling straight at me! I swear I did one hundred meters in nine point nine seconds. I smashed out of the trees and leaped down the bank in three bounds.

Maura-Lee was calmly walking along the tracks. "The dog won't come this far," she said.

"Have you lost your marbles? That was the garbage man's dog! The man who burned down his house and killed his family!"

She glared at me, her dark eyes sparking. "Are you totally *stupid?* Do you believe *everything* you hear?"

"No! I don't believe you can read minds."

Her jaw jutted out. She looked ready to explode, then turned and walked away.

CHAPTER 13

Eight Dollars

My heart rate slowly dropped to normal. We had a trout. A *big* trout. The petrel would eat well.

I cleared my throat. "It's not nice to call someone stupid."

"A rose by any other name ..."

"Well, in our house we don't use the word 'stupid'."

"Okay, how about 'brain cell–challenged'?"

"That's good. I hadn't thought of that one."

She looked at me sideways. "What *have* you thought of?"

I shrugged. "The usual stuff. Not the sharpest knife in the drawer. Hamster fell off the wheel ..."

"Frankie Uccello, your hamster's *dead.* You're too weird!"

I smiled. I couldn't help myself. "You should know."

Maura-Lee stopped, scanned me from sneakers to shoulder. Then to my surprise she smiled. "I didn't say weird was bad. It's way better than *normal.* Normal is *boring.*"

"Yeah," I replied. "Sure is."

We crossed the bridge. "Here's your stu— brain cell–challenged fish," she said briskly. "You better get it cleaned and in the fridge right away. I'm going back to school."

"See ya," I said. "And thanks." I took the bag and headed straight up College Street and through several backyards to home. Pookey was glad to see me and begged to help me dispose of the fish guts, which I wrapped in newspaper along with the remains of the perch and stuffed in the compost bin. Then I stowed the rainbow trout in a container and buried it at the back of the fridge.

The petrel looked comfortable, huddled against the water bowl with its head up and bill resting against its dark chest feathers. It seemed to be still sleeping off breakfast.

I ran all the way back to school, hoping no one had noticed I'd gone AWOL — two days in a row was beyond pushing my luck. I made it just as recess was ending. Mrs. Rose was talking to Bomb in the foyer. She nodded as I came inside. Bomb ignored me. I relaxed. No one had noticed.

A punch landed between my shoulder blades. "Holy horse's hiney! Are you out of your flipping skull?"

I had to laugh. "I'm not the one saying 'Holy horse's hiney' in public. What's up, Tim?"

"What's up? I'll tell you what's up! Three oranges, four zucchinis and eight pumpkins! Way up! We wait four freaking years for that—" He looked back at Bomb and squeezed his volume down to a high-pitched hiss. "—and *you missed it!* Where *were* you?"

What was I supposed to say? That I snuck out of school, killed a huge trout with a rock and nearly got run down by the garbage man's Rottweiler? Put that way, it *was* a great story, and Tim loved stories — he could probably make a living telling stories. But he was good at digging out all the gory details. Maura-Lee was a gory detail.

"Something came up."

Tim squinted at me. "You know I'll find out. You might as well tell me your version first. See you at lunch." It was almost a threat.

As I entered my next class, Maura-Lee looked down at her open scribbler. I wondered if she would really go back to the U-fish. She had been there before, for sure. Did the garbage man live there? Wasn't she afraid of the dog? Even if that Rottweiler was anchored to a three-ton tow chain, *I* wouldn't go back there again.

Mrs. Rose came in. "Open your books to chapter twelve. I hope you all read it last night."

I had a hard time with history. Names of places and people refused to be digested, like I had an allergy to words that started with a capital letter. Not Maura-Lee. She never flubbed a question.

After class, as the herd crowded down the hallway to the cafeteria, Maura-Lee appeared. "Don't forget to bring eight dollars tonight."

"So you're going back to the U-fish?"

"I'm not a thief!"

"But the dog ..."

"He's usually tied up." She didn't look worried.

"*Usually* is no guarantee."

She just shrugged. "Don't forget."

I nodded before I remembered what I was nodding about. Hug a Horse Farm. I wasn't planning on going back there. But, just yesterday I wasn't planning on going near Maura-Lee, either. I couldn't stick to a plan with a bucket of glue. She was right. I was beyond brain cell–challenged.

And I didn't have eight dollars. I'd just spent my last penny on the perch. I'd have to hit the guys for a loan. If I could pay Maura-Lee that afternoon I could avoid going to Hug a Horse.

At lunch I got a detailed, and probably exaggerated, play-by-play of Blastoff. Tim and Mike relived every smoke-filled, eardrum-smashing moment. When they finally got it out of their systems and I was feeling like I had missed living, I asked if I could borrow eight dollars.

"I'm broke," said Mike.

Tim said, "I only have two toonies." He plunked the coins on the table. "But I could bring the rest tonight."

I chewed my lip in frustration.

"What's bugging you?" asked Tim.

"I was hoping not to go," I said.

"You have to!"

"Joey got on the horse. He doesn't need me anymore."

"Need you for what?" asked Mike.

"Uh-uh," said Tim. "Susan won't let anyone ride without *both* siderunners. You don't show, Joey doesn't ride. And we never hear the end of it. Literally."

"The end of what?" Mike insisted.

Tim grinned. "Frankie actually rode a *horse* Monday night."

"No kidding?" said Mike. "Which one?"

"A black one," I grumbled.

Mike's jaw dropped. "Not that huge thing of Kim's! Even I wouldn't get on him!"

Tim chuckled. "No, not The Ghost. Maura-Lee has a much smaller horse."

"Maura-Lee?" Mike asked. "*Weird* Maura-Lee?"

Tim nodded.

"Figures," said Mike, enjoying himself way too much. "All you horse people are loony tunes."

"Watch it, Cow-patty!" Tim wadded up his napkin and drilled it at Mike's head.

Mike ducked. "Not that that's a bad thing. I was considering buying a horse myself ... seeing as all those horsy girls you hang out with are so good-looking. Can't let Tim get them all, eh, Frankie? So what's Maura-Lee like?"

"Prince is her first horse," said Tim, "so she doesn't ride very well, but it's uncanny how fast she —"

Mike cut him off. "No, man. What is she *like?*"

"I thought you had a thing for Lana."

"Out of my league. But if Maura-Lee's into big animals" — he slapped his chest and spread his arms — "I'm available! And she's darn cute once you get past weird. Frankie, I saw you talking to her. So you think she'd go for me, or what?"

Instead of being concerned for Mike's loss of sanity, Tim looked baffled. "Maura-Lee actually talked to

Frankie? I've never heard her say a word to anyone in school except teachers since ... since *forever*." He frowned at me. "So what are you two up to?"

"It's not 'you two' and don't you go — "

The end-of-lunch buzzer never sounded so sweet. "Got to run." I hauled out of there without even a "see you later." I never felt so uncomfortable around Tim and Mike before. Why didn't I just tell them what was going on?

The answer hid in wings and dreams and a weird feeling in the pit of my stomach.

The rest of the day was dull. The teachers didn't work too hard. They knew they'd been outdone by Cannon. After school Tim almost missed his bus nagging me about Hug a Horse Farm. He could be such an old woman.

The petrel eagerly scarfed back another pile of fish slivers, then snuggled its head under one wing and settled back to sleep. I grinned until my cheeks hurt. I thought about how petrels nested in underground burrows, and wondered if the cardboard box and dark closet felt familiar and comforting.

I sat there for ages, following the rise and fall of each tiny breath, mesmerized by the endless shades of blacks and browns sifting through the interlaced feathers. I found myself praying, "Please let this one fly away. Please. Just this one. It's not a big job. Just one little bird. Please. *Please.*"

I wouldn't be able to get to the trout in the kitchen later without being caught, so I cut up some more, wrapped it in a plastic bag and stashed it in my room. Bernie clomped down to the family room and turned her version of music on so loud the floor throbbed. I brought my homework up to the dining room table. An hour later Dad roared in, thumped his helmet on the kitchen counter and started unloading the dishwasher. Then Mom came home, looking like she'd been trampled by a herd of wild seven-year-olds, which was entirely possible.

"Oh, the little *darlings.*" "Darlings" sounded like it was a four-letter word. "I knew building the elementary school next to the junior school was a mistake. The kids spent the whole day fighting over how many fruit went to the moon."

"Three oranges, four zucchinis and eight pumpkins," I said.

"Hi, Frankie, dear." She sighed, and groaned at Dad. "They came that close" — she held her thumb and forefinger tight together — "to driving me insane!"

"You could get a different job," said Dad.

"But teaching is my bliss!"

"So what are your students? Your bliss-ters?"

Mom groaned again, only with a smile this time. "So what's for supper?"

Dad grimaced. "On nights like this I really do wish I knew how to cook."

"You could learn."

"I'd just burn everything."

"You're right. And I don't mind cooking. I just hate trying to think of *what* to cook every night of my life."

"What you need is a Meal of Fortune," Dad said dramatically, perfectly imitating the TV announcer. "Spin the wheel. See what's for supper tonight."

Mom laughed. "What if it lands on Super Leftover Surprise, an all-expense-paid dinner for four at the exclusive Uccello Resort?"

"Then Super Leftover Surprise it is." Dad spread his arms and Mom dove in for a Melter.

When they were through, I asked, "Can I borrow eight dollars?"

"I thought you had quite a bit saved up," said Mom.

"I had to buy some new wheel trucks." And perch, but I didn't say that.

"Oh, Frankie, how many times do I have to tell you not to buy stuff for yourself *right before your birthday?* Or Christmas ... or anniversary." She whacked Dad on the back.

"What'd *I* do?" Dad protested.

"You men, you're all alike. Frankie, what am I supposed to buy you for your birthday, now that I can't buy you wheel trucks?"

"Anything but clothes," Dad muttered.

"Hey! I gave you that shirt you have on and *never* take off!"

"And I lo-o-ve it," said Dad, ducking another whack.

Mom fished eight dollars from her purse. Then her head disappeared into the depths of the fridge. "Super Leftover Surprise coming right up," she said, as she emerged with a pile of containers — including my trout.

CHAPTER 14

Colors

I braced for the let-nature-take-its-course lecture. Then Dad said, "You know, Hon. You're right. It's *my* turn to cook."

"But Bob — "

"No arguments!" He quickly stuffed all the containers back in the fridge and picked up the car keys. "Back in a sec."

Mom looked at me, and her eyebrows bobbed up and down. "Pizza!"

Bernie rocketed up the basement stairs. "No mushrooms!" she shouted after Dad.

Mom laughed. "She could *not* have heard me. She's got pizza ESP."

Thirty-five minutes later there was nothing left but two greasy boxes and the fragrance of pepperoni and tomato sauce. Dad checked his watch. "Riding tonight, Frankie."

I groaned.

Dad nearly jumped down my throat. "When you volunteer for something, you follow it through. To the end!"

"*You're* the one that volunteered me!"

"And you did great. Jean, did I tell you? Susan said Frankie actually rode a *horse* on Monday."

Mom beamed at me. "There now, aren't you glad your father signed you up?"

The sun backlit the greens and golds along the hills to Meadow Green. Each leaf and blade of grass shone like stained glass. At Hug a Horse Farm, the parking area was empty.

"Maybe it was cancelled," I said, hoping beyond hope.

"Can't be. I talked to Susan this afternoon. She offered to drive you home again. Out you get."

I walked to the brown barn and peeked inside. Nothing alive in there except a squirrel. It bolted up a stall wall and hung off a horse-shaped sign that read "The Ghost Horse of Meadow Green" in hand-painted green letters. I clucked back at the squirrel's scolding chirps and headed for the indoor arena. As I neared, I heard a voice, loud and annoyed. "Prince, PRINCE! Pay attention!"

I walked silently up behind the bleachers with the red jacket on top. Maura-Lee stood at the far end of the arena; Prince was walking straight away from her. She marched forward and clapped her hands. "Prince!" Prince's ears rotated slightly, but he continued straight into the corner. There he stopped, slowly raised his tail, grunted and dumped a huge steamer followed by an endless rattling fart.

I chuckled. Maura-Lee jumped. She glared at me, then at the horse, and let out a shoulder-sagging sigh. "He's not supposed to ignore me like that," she said.

"Looks to me like he just doesn't want to poop where he walks. I wouldn't."

She looked at me like I had no right to an opinion, but said, "Yeah, maybe. You're early. It doesn't start until 7:30 on Wednesdays."

"Nice of someone to tell me."

Prince turned his head and pointed his short fuzzy ears at Maura-Lee, giving her a long, big-eyed stare.

"You old dope," she said to him. "I can't stay mad when you're so cute." She moved toward his belly. "*Walk on.*" Her horse turned back his ears and walked in a wide arc around her.

"He looks angry," I said.

"No, angry is ears pinned flat. Those are 'I don't want to but I will anyway' ears."

When Prince's circle came alongside the bleachers, he stopped and gave me a look. Two days ago that look would have generated scenes of extreme violence — viewer discretion advised — but I realized my fear was way down to a PG rating. And the bit of tongue sticking out the side of his mouth actually made me smile.

"What's wrong with his tongue?" I asked.

"Nothing. He has a crooked lip. It lets the tongue fall out. It's genetic.

"Prince, walk on," Maura-Lee said firmly. Prince swiveled one ear and lazily did what he was told, barely lifting the toes of his hooves to clear the sand. After another circle, Maura-Lee called, "And whoa." Prince stopped and turned to face her. His tongue disappeared and his mouth moved like he was eating.

"Good boy!" Maura-Lee crowed, as if he'd just done the trick of the century. She walked up and kissed the short fluffy fur behind his ears. "Chewing like that means he's being submissive. You can pat him if you want."

"No, thank you."

"He won't hurt you. When he looked at you his ears were forward and his neck was level. That's friendly posture. Bossy is neck high and stiff. Nasty is neck level but nose out and ears pinned. He likes you."

"You sound pretty sure."

"His body doesn't lie ... and he's pink." She said this matter-of-factly — like it made sense.

"Pink?"

She looked across the mass of wavy mane draped down both sides of the horse's thick neck. "When Prince is near you, he's pink ... I mean, I see pink. Pink means he likes you."

Maura-Lee had a strange sense of humor. I played along. "The way he was batting those long eyelashes at me, I thought he loved me."

"No, then I'd see red."

"Doesn't 'seeing red' mean anger?"

"No," she said, impatiently. "Anger is black"

Okay, all aboard the train to Weirdsville. I watched her stroke the horse's muzzle, where his black-brown fur blended into rich reddish-brown above his nostrils. "You see an aura, or something?"

"Not exactly. More like pink squiggles all over him."

"So you know what he's thinking?"

She shook her head. "Just what he's feeling." There was a challenge in her eyes.

Why was she telling *me* this stuff? Seeing colors. That was pretty weird. That was like ...

Then I realized what it was like. I saw colors ... in my dreams.

"So-o-o," I asked nervously, "can you tell what I'm thinking ... I mean, feeling?"

She nodded. "Except when the colors get all muzzy."

Maura-Lee was chatting calmly, like we were having a conversation about the weather. "Prince has been very gray lately, which means he's feeling sad. I think he misses his old family. Especially the girl he used to own."

"You mean the girl who used to own *him?*"

"No. Vanessa thinks he was used to being the boss."

"Then how can you make him do that stuff?"

"I don't *make* him. I *ask* him, but in a way that gets him to want to say yes. In the wild, horses spend all day trying to eat and not get eaten. The boss of the herd knows where to find food and when to run from predators. I have to act like the boss, and if Prince believes it, he'll move when I say move and stop when I say stop, 'cause I'm keeping him safe.

"Trouble is Prince knows I don't always know what I'm doing. It's really hard."

"Then why do you do it?"

She patted Prince's forehead where scattered white hairs circled above each eye. He moved his jaw and licked his lips. "Why did *you* rescue the petrel?"

I shrugged. "I like birds?"

"A lot of people *like* birds."

It was as if a door had blown open and I couldn't push it shut. I heard myself say, "And I had this dream."

Once I started talking, I didn't stop until I had told her all about my flying dream. And then I was so nerved up I blabbed about the turquoise dream and how Nanna had died three days later and that's when I got my idea and, after the flying dream, I found the petrel so I figured it was true.

"I think I can dream the future."

It came out just like that! Like it had been waiting. I mean, it was the biggest thing in my life, my *one* talent. The one thing that finally made me special. I had to tell *someone* before my brain exploded. Besides Maura-Lee had told me *her* secret.

But when I was done, I sputtered, "I don't know why I told you that. I guess you think I'm pretty weird."

She looked at me carefully and said, "Maybe your dream was black *and* red." She stroked Prince's neck. "But you didn't dream the *future* if the petrel's accident happened the night you were dreaming."

CHAPTER 15

A Problem

Black *and* red. My brain got all knotted up and before I could untangle it Tim appeared in the doorway. I suddenly felt naked, like in those dreams where you're in school without your pants. What if Maura-Lee said something? What if …

"I won't say anything if you don't," Maura-Lee whispered.

Tim strolled over. "Aren't you an eager beaver?" he said, grinning his bright-toothed smile.

"You could have told me it started late on Wednesdays."

Kim limped in, the usual Hug a Horse smile missing.

"What happened?" asked Tim.

"Jelly Bean stepped on my foot."

"Ouch! You have to pay attention around her."

"*She's* the one that wasn't paying attention. She walked right into me!" Then she laughed. "You should have seen the look on her face when I hollered."

"Are you sure you're okay to work tonight?"

"Yeah, I think so."

Maura-Lee buckled a halter on Prince and led him outside just as the Freestar and a spotless white Pathfinder rolled up. The girls all said a cheerful hi, except Patsy. "My turn to get the horses," she said coldly, and dragged a chill into the barn ahead of Maura-Lee and Prince.

As Prince's square butt disappeared, Lana said, "Someone has to talk to Maura-Lee. She went after Patsy in school today."

"She hit her?" asked Tim.

"No, she did that impersonation thing again. Patsy was mortified."

Michelle nodded. "It'd be totally better if she *did* hit her. That other thing is ... is ..."

"Probably the most brilliant passive-aggressive behavior I've ever seen," I said.

The girls all looked at me like I had just landed from Mars, but Tim nodded. "That fits. Maura-Lee doesn't express her emotions very well."

"She does 'angry' just fine," said Lana.

"Maybe Frankie should talk to her," said Tim. "Seemed pretty friendly when I arrived."

"She was just teaching me some stuff about horses."

"But the Maura-Lee we know is even quieter than Kim here."

Kim silently agreed.

Tim shrugged his bony shoulders. "Well, time to get the ponies ready. Hop to it, you slackers!"

I stayed by the front door of the barn. Patsy already had Strawberry tied in the aisle and was leading in Belle ... or maybe Fleur. "What took you guys so long?" she grumbled, "Do I have to do everything around here?"

Lana rolled her eyes but smiled. "Sorry, Patsy."

The activity and noise piled up fast. Fleur ... or maybe Belle ... was led in, leaving The Ghost, Star and some fuzzy little white pony hanging over the back-door gate. Prince was tied nearest me. Maura-Lee appeared with a saddle hugged to her chest and a bridle in one fist.

"Here, hold this." She passed me the bridle. As she buckled Prince's girth, he kept giving me those looks. Tim kept shaking his head at me and chuckling.

When the riders arrived, I backed outside. I was doing okay — heart rate reasonably normal, no excessive sweating — until everyone marched to the arena and mounted their horses ... except for Joey.

"You first," he said to me, rhythmically waving. "You first."

"But you did fine last time. You know how to ride now."

"You first. You first. You first."

I took a deep breath — belly, chest, shoulders. Okay, okay. You've done this once ... Prince blasted a nostrilful of wet snot right in my face. I jumped back, but the real shock was that I only reacted to the wet spray and not to some thought of being stomped on!

Mary and Charlotte thought it was hilarious and laughed loudly. I smiled. I strapped on a helmet and placed my foot (the correct one) in the stirrup. That's when my body started to shake. I couldn't stop it. I barely had the strength to throw my leg over the horse. The instant I felt the saddle under me, a sense of helplessness the size of a school bus grabbed me. What if Prince got away from Maura-Lee? What if he took off?

"You won't let go, will you?" I hissed to Maura-Lee.

"Of course not. Prince, walk on."

Prince started to move. My fear rocked and flexed ... and softened. My seat bones walked on the saddle leather, left, right, left, right. It wasn't so bad!

"He doesn't seem as tall this time," I said.

"He's *not* tall, only 14.1 hands, a pony according to the rules. But he's a horse breed. A purebred Cheval Canadien. They're usually short but strong. The Little Iron Horse. They're a very old breed, from horses sent to Quebec by King Louis XIV of France in the sixteen hundreds. Fleur and Belle are Canadiens, too." She looked back at me. "You're doing better."

"Yeah, I guess. If you weren't there, how would I stop him?"

"I just pull on the reins a bit and lean back. But I'm not good at stopping yet. He doesn't always listen."

"That's comforting."

"While I'm riding, not leading. I only started taking riding lessons. You could take lessons, too, if you want. On Prince. He really does like you."

"He's pink again, is he?" The image of me on a pink horse bumped into my nervousness and I started to chuckle. I couldn't help myself. Me, Frankie, cool skater dude riding a *pink* horse. By the time we came back around to the group by the door I was laughing so hard tears trickled off my chin, and a giggle bubbled from Maura-Lee.

Tim looked at us like we were both two bricks short of a load. That made me laugh more. I wondered what color laughter was.

Then Joey required my full attention, and a long hour followed. The steady plod of hooves, creaking saddles, Susan's boisterous directions and Mary's chatter melted into a blur. I still held my breath past the freshest steamers, but I actually enjoyed the earthy scent of damp sand and warm horses. The only outburst from Joey was an over-happy spell of shouting. Maura-Lee had been right about Prince, though; he wasn't fazed a bit. He just tightened his ears down sideways and ambled along.

When all the riders had dismounted, everyone paraded back to the barn except for Maura-Lee. She had a very serious look on her face.

"Did I do something wrong?" I asked.

Maura-Lee blinked at me. "No. I was just thinking about Prince."

"He behaved well tonight," I said. Then I remembered the eight dollars in my pocket. "Here's the money for the trout. The petrel sure does like it."

"Good," she said flatly. She took off Prince's tack, set it on the bleachers and put on her jacket. Then she led her horse to the far end of the arena and put her shoulder to the sliding back door. She and Prince disappeared outside and the door closed behind them just as Tim walked in.

He faked a punch at my stomach. "You dog, you! Got on a horse *again!* We'll make a rider out of you yet."

"In your dreams!"

"Want to walk down to my place? I've got that new game card plugged in with double the RAM. You should see that baby perform! Dad could drive you home."

"Can't. School night."

"Okay. You on-line later?"

I shook my head. "Bernie's got the computer tonight."

Hug a Horse Farm cleared out in a quiet hurry. Everyone waved happy-tired good-byes. Susan said she'd be just a minute and went into the house with Vanessa. I leaned against the brown barn wall letting the heat of the day's sun warm my back. There wasn't a breath of wind, and I swear I could feel the dew settling on my nose. It was really beautiful and peaceful. So why was I feeling down?

The *whoosh, whoosh* of large feathers made me look up; two crows swooped and rolled over the farm. I envied that power of flight. Then my mind flew to the petrel and I remembered Maura-Lee had said that the petrel's accident wasn't in the future — it was on the night of my dream.

That was it, wasn't it? The wings, the red rider — not the future, just my imagination. The petrel just one enormous coincidence.

Okay, not even an *enormous* coincidence. There were tons of black-winged birds.

And my turquoise dream? My whole family knew Nanna was on the way out. Dreaming about saying good-bye was no stretch. And no talent. Only people like Maura-Lee had secret talents to go with all their other talents. It wasn't fair. It was never fair.

The air suddenly vibrated with a high-pitched squeal. Then another, followed by a thud.

Something is wrong!

The roof of the arena reflected the sunset, its silver steel transformed to red — dream-red! *Thud, thud, thud* from the far side of the arena.

Where were the horses?

Where was Maura-Lee?

Another pinched-off squeal, desperate. Something was really wrong! Was Maura-Lee in trouble? The house was too far away to get help. I had to *do* something! I ran through the barn, grabbed a long-handled shovel and ducked through the boards.

A clamped-down scream came from the far side of the arena. I raised the shovel and hurried toward it.

Then the words, "I HATE you! I HATE you! You're STUPID! STUPID, STUPID, STUPID!" and a continuous whacking sound. I rounded the corner. Maura-Lee was huddled against the steel wall, knees tight to her chest. The fuzzy white pony loomed over her, its mouth in her face. She elbowed it back and struck the sides of her head hard with both palms, over and over and over. "Stupid, stupid, stupid, stupid!" she grunted. *Whack, whack, whack, whack.*

"Stop!" I gasped. "What's wrong?"

"NOTHING!" she screamed, and covered her head with her arms. "EVERYTHING! GO AWAY!"

The pony started licking her left hand with long wet strokes of its pink tongue, pushing up her sleeve, slobbering along gnarled white scars on her wrist. She jerked the sleeve back down and screamed again, "GO AWAY! GO AWAY!"

She wasn't screaming at the pony.

I went away — to the barn, through the boards, out the front door. I propped the shovel against the brown wall.

Susan was walking up from the house. "You ready to go?"

I nodded. Ready to go and never come back.

CHAPTER 16

The Talk

All the way home I saw Maura-Lee huddled against the arena wall — with its sudden-red roof and her in her red jacket — hitting her head.

The red rider in my dream.

Well, not really. You can find coincidences in anything if you try hard enough. Maura-Lee wasn't riding a black horse. And she didn't fall.

But she owns a black horse. And she was at a big arena with a red roof.

No. No. No.

Mom and Dad were out for their evening walk. Good. No "How did it go tonight?" conversation. I shoved the world out of my head and settled down with the petrel. The bird happily gulped back the trout and stood steady on both feet. Pale thin eyelids like grandmother skin blinked slowly over its tiny black eyes. It looked around, head moving in short, start-stop action like a small soft robot. My heart smiled.

I studied the feathers, layer after layer of dark brown, gray-brown, black-brown, all different, so intricate, so perfect.

"How many miles of ocean have you seen? Were you flying south when the storm caught you? You'll be able to go real soon. How about some exercise, to get in shape for your big day?"

I shut the window blinds so the bird wouldn't fly into the glass, then bulldozed open an area at the foot of my bed. Gently cupping both hands around the warm body, I lifted it out of the box and set it free on the rug. The little fellow craned its neck and tilted its head, looking at the ceiling — or the floor, hard to say which. I gave its tail feathers a nudge with my toe. It walked around, pecked a dirt spot on the carpet, but kept its wings firmly shut.

"How about a little flying?" I picked it up and gently tossed it onto my bed. The dark wings flicked open at the last instant, barely preventing a crash landing on the blankets.

"I'm sorry, I guess you weren't expecting that."

I held the bird up again, a little webbed foot pressing lightly on each palm. Then I quickly dropped my hands just a bit. The wings popped opened for balance. I raised and repeated, and each time the wings opened. On the fifth drop I said, "Okay, off you go," and tossed it toward the bed. This time its wings stayed out, slightly bent, and it sort of glided into a heap on my pillow.

"No!" I grumbled. "You're supposed to go *up*, not *down*."

I heard Mom and Dad thump in the back door.

"The morning will be better," I told the petrel. "Another good night's sleep and you'll do it." One more night. I put the bird back in its box.

What if it doesn't fly?

Dad called down the stairs, "Are you in, Frankie? How'd it go at Hug a Horse tonight?"

An unexpected tsunami of anger rolled over me. "*Fine!*" It was all Dad's fault! If it weren't for his messing with my life, I wouldn't have been there tonight. And if Susan had just gone home on time, I wouldn't have seen what I saw.

I fell on my bed and punched my pillow. Why can't everyone just leave me alone?

A soft knock on my door and Mom asked, "Are you okay?"

"*Yes.*"

"Did you have a fight with one of your friends?"

"*No!*"

"Did something scare you?"

"*NO!*"

"Are you sure? You know how your father gets angry when he's scared. Maybe you should talk about it."

"I don't need to talk."

"All right. I'll be upstairs."

How could I talk? Dad would be page after page of clichés. And Mom, well, sometimes she was okay, but about a *girl?* She'd go all gushy — how did her little boy grow up so fast — want all the details, and then tell Dad to repeat that sex talk thing again! Hopeless! No, if I talked it would have to be a person who couldn't care less if I lived or died. Bernie.

I went into the family room. Bernie was typing a conversation into some chat room or other.

"It's my night to use the computer," she said.

"I know."

She tapped out a few more sentences and hit the back-in-a-minute icon. "So what's her name?"

"Huh?"

"Well, you won't talk to Mom so this is about a girl, right?"

Reluctantly I nodded.

"And you want to ask her out."

"No!"

"She's asked you out?"

"NO!"

"Sorry," said Bernie.

What was I doing here?

Bernie picked up a pen and twirled it in her fingers. "Is she in your class?"

"Yeah."

"And ..."

"And," I repeated slowly. "And ... she's the smartest kid in ninth grade and she's got truckloads of talent and ... "

"Like me," said Bernie, with an over-wide smile.

I rolled my eyes and got up. "I knew I shouldn't have — "

"Hold on. I'm sorry." She actually meant it. "And what?"

"And ... she hates herself."

"How do you know?"

"She said so."

"Heck, all teenage girls hate themselves at least twice a week."

"Do they hit themselves on the head ... *hard* ... over and over?"

Bernie put the pen down. "Whoa! So do you think she's going to hurt herself more? Is she suicidal?"

I hadn't thought about that. Then I remembered the scars on her wrist. I told Bernie. She chewed her lip for a bit, and said, "It probably wasn't a suicide attempt. Stuff like that gets around and you'd have heard. Maybe she's a cutter."

I shrugged.

"You have to tell someone."

"Yeah? Like who?"

"Her mother? That would be my first choice."

"Yeah, I guess."

"Your guidance counselor? Who do you have this year?"

"The Claw."

"They still let him near kids? The way he squeezes shoulders and breathes right in your face — he totally creeps me out."

"You and everyone else."

Bernie was quiet for a long time. "There's a kids

help line at the hospital." She typed into the computer, found the number and wrote the information on a piece of yellow paper. "You could call and ask for advice or give this to your friend and let her decide what to do."

I took the paper.

Mom came downstairs with a load of laundry. "Feeling better?"

"Yeah."

"How's your project going, Bernie?" she asked, checking the computer screen.

Bernie had brought up a window with several bright-colored graphs. "I've discovered there's a direct correlation between good marks and the food choices kids make in the cafeteria."

"Oh, Bernie," Mom gushed, "you're so amazing."

Bernie smiled. If she was so smart why didn't she know it was just a parent's job to say that stuff? I snorted.

Mom said, "Frankie, if you would just apply yourself, you'd be amazing, too," which proved my point. Mom tried to kiss my forehead. I dodged and escaped to my room.

I tucked the piece of yellow paper into the side pocket of my backpack and sneaked a peek at the petrel. It heard me and stretched up tall. Its wings opened up and out and wide and beautiful. They hit the air with three quick beats. Then it wiggled its tail and folded itself back to sleep.

"I saw that! Those wings work! No excuse tomorrow. You're going to fly!"

I fell asleep smiling, my head full of soaring wings.

And woke up laughing.

I had dreamed I was riding a horse down a country road. And everything was blue, royal blue — the crushed mailbox I passed, a car coming toward me, even the horse. I was riding a royal-blue horse. And right there in the middle of my dream, I knew it was a *color dream,* so I ordered myself to pay attention. Then there was this ridiculous screaming like in a bad horror movie and the horse walked right over the car! Then it wasn't a car but a four-wheeler, and the driver was Slug and he had this look of misery and fear all mashed into one! That's when I knew this was the screwiest dream I'd ever had, and I started to laugh. And I woke up.

Something is wrong.

Ha! Darn right something's wrong. That dream was nuts! Horses don't run over cars. And Slug scared? Totally nuts. Proof positive that my color dreams were just my pathetic hyperactive imagination playing jokes on me.

I was relieved. Dreaming the future meant responsibilities. Normal was a heck of a lot easier.

That's when my alarm went off. I whacked the button and hurried upstairs to get the fish out of the fridge before anyone else was up. "This feeding thing is getting tedious," I complained to the petrel, as it stood tall, waiting for breakfast. All I had to do was place my finger and thumb on either side of the narrow, black beak and it opened. The dainty creature pigged out and then scurried around my bedroom with such energy I had to laugh. Its amazing recovery made me feel so good I decided to head to school early. I'd go uphill instead of down, same distance, but I might catch Maura-Lee to give her that phone number. What could it hurt? Bernie *might* be right. Maura-Lee might even call the number and maybe get some help.

A soft drizzle punched up the early fall colors. Purple and yellow flowers shouted from doorsteps, but could barely be heard over whole trees of blaring reds and oranges.

At the corner of Xavier Drive I waited on the sidewalk, trying to beat my distance record for manuals. I didn't — my grip tape needed replacing and my right foot kept slipping — but I messed around with kickflips (four brilliant ones), landing solid and square. On the fifth the worn tape kept my toe from dragging the nose over. I credit-carded myself and collapsed in the wet grass gulping for breath and trying not to lose my breakfast.

Maybe Maura-Lee got a drive. Maybe she was going past at the moment I was clocking myself in the nuts. I gave up.

I made it to school a little late. I was still half green so Mrs. Rose didn't give me a hard time.

Maura-Lee never showed.

CHAPTER 17

Cooked

It wasn't my fault Maura-Lee didn't come to school, so why did I suddenly feel like a speeding car heading for an accident? When Slug slammed down the hall after first class, pounding locker doors with his fist to see how much noise he could make, all I could do was stare, remembering the look on his face in my dream.

"What are you looking at?"

"Nothing. Nothing at all."

I turned my back on him and marched into class. Roddie was using my seat as a footstool. I kicked it out from under his huge sneakers and sat down as far from Cannon as the walls would let me. Not far enough. When Cannon started talking, for the first time I heard what he was really saying. His "for all of us interested in rare bird sightings" really meant "for anyone like him with an obsession for lists and numbers and no concern for the bird." That morning he eagerly reported on some poor crane blown from the southern States by the storm. What he didn't say was how it would never find its way home and never survive our northern winter. Cannon's "amazing bit of luck" was the bird's slow, sad death.

At recess Tim and Mike jumped me from behind the staircase with a double whoop and tackle. I never won against Tim's height and Mike's muscle, but fought back anyway. Mike held my head under his armpit a moment too long and I thumped him hard in the solar plexus. As he gulped for air, Tim chuckled.

"I got the perfect birthday present for you, Frankie," he boasted.

"You got a birthday coming up?" asked Mike, still wheezing.

"Yeah, Saturday."

"And I'm going to give him something he's *never* had before." Tim grinned — his old cat-ate-the-goldfish grin.

"What if it's something I already have?"

"Not a chance!"

"My birthday's on a Thursday this year," said Mike. "Auction day! Dad's taking me to Truro and I can bid on any cow I want!" It wasn't so much what he said as *how* he said it — like the prettiest girl in school had just asked him out. Tim nearly fell down laughing and, I confess, I cracked a smile.

"Hey, I don't pick on you about your dumb horses!" Mike protested and toppled Tim into a passing huddle of seventh-grade girls.

"So, Frankie, what are you going to wish for when you blow out the candles on your cake? I'm thinking fate owes me a date with Lana. It's worth a try."

"Good thing you didn't say you were going to wish for another cow," said Tim. "Frankie and I would've had to pound you."

Mike grinned. "But I'm *getting* another cow. So what's *your* wish, Frankie?"

"He can't make a wish," said Tim. "He never gets candles."

I looked daggers at Tim but it was too late.

"*No* candles?" Mike exclaimed. "What's a birthday cake without candles?"

"It's a tradition," I grumbled.

"Uh-uh." Mike shook his head. "*Candles* are the tradition."

"Not for Frankie," said Tim, avoiding my glare. There was a story to be told and Tim's skin was going to peel off and his insides fall out if he didn't get a chance to tell it. "When he was five years old his mom brought out his birthday cake with the candles lit," said Tim, talking so fast he nearly tripped over his tongue. "Frankie screamed and ran out the door and wouldn't come back in the house even to open his presents! We ended up having the party in the backyard. It was raining and we all hid under umbrellas and the frosting got washed right off the cake before we finished eating it and — "

"Come on. Even *I* don't remember all that!"

Tim shrugged. "It was cool."

"So how come you ran?" asked Mike.

"How should I know? I was a little kid." But I *did* know. The night before my fifth birthday I had had the orange dream.

"So what are my chances?" asked Mike. "Does Lana have a thing for anyone?"

I could have told Mike how she'd been chasing Tim all summer, but then I'd have to listen to Tim denying it. He was totally blind to her, and clearly interested in someone else, only I hadn't figured out who.

Tim replied, "I don't think so."

Mike nodded. "Good!" His expression suddenly darkened. "Oh, I forgot to tell you," he said to Tim. "Slug got himself a four-wheeler."

I nearly choked on my orange juice.

You dreamed about Slug on a four-wheeler!

The dream didn't mean anything — Slug's been bragging about buying a four-wheeler for ages.

"You okay?" Mike asked, and slapped me on the back.

Tim looked miffed that Mike had a story before he did. "Who told you that?"

"Saw him going like an idiot through St. Andrews. Not even a helmet on."

"No need for a helmet," said Tim. "Nothing to protect."

"Well, watch out for him. He was barely in control."

"Yeah, thanks for the warning."

Mike then launched into the details of the repairs he and his dad made to the milk-house roof and the manure scraper or spreader or whatever. My brain was suddenly very tired and I tuned out for the rest of the afternoon.

After school the wind was sharp and cold, so I yanked out my extra T-shirt from the side pocket of my backpack. The yellow paper blew out. Tim stomped on it with his size thirteens, read it and handed it back.

"I'm a good listener."

"Since when?" I crammed the paper into my pocket.

"When I stop talking." He looked worried.

"It's *not* for me." I pushed my board for home, ambushed by the thought I'd avoided all day. Maura-Lee *never* missed school. Was she sick? Did she hurt herself last night? I mean, hurt herself *more?* After I saw her? After I just walked away?

She told me to go. What was I supposed to do? It wasn't my fault.

I blasted down the sidewalk, carving hard around a group of college students. "Watch it, punk," a big guy shouted, but I didn't care. They were in my way. Everyone was in my way.

The petrel wolfed down all the trout I'd cut up and I had to go back to the kitchen for more. I had just buried the container back in the fridge when the thump of Mom's car door announced she was home early. I booted it down to my room. A bit later Mom called down, "Frankie, supper will be at five tonight. Your dad and I have to go to the Gillises' anniversary party."

"Fine by me." That would give me lots of time to take the petrel to the Landing and set it free.

I finished feeding it and tried the drop-drop-toss

thing again. It glided perfectly to my pillow. Down. Not up. Not one hint of flying. Not one wing beat. Nada. Zip.

"Please, little fella. One more time, eh? Give it all you got."

All I got was juicy poop sprayed across my pile of once-worn clothes. I put the petrel back in the closet. "Okay. I'm rushing things. Tomorrow. You'll fly tomorrow."

I heard the *chug-chug-uh* of Dad's Goldwing shutting down. Mom shouted, "Supper's almost ready." I suddenly didn't feel like eating but dragged myself up to the kitchen anyway. Something popped and sizzled in the frying pan. Mom said cheerfully, "Frankie, yours is in the microwave."

Dad came in the back door and Mom jumped on him with a tight Monkey hug. "You big lug! You'd do anything to avoid Super Leftover Surprise. When were you going to tell me you bought my favorite fish?"

"I did?" Dad waddled them both over to the stove. "Man, that's some trout!"

"Trout? NO!" I yanked the pan off the heat. "You can't cook that!"

Mom let go of Dad and poked the golden, flour-encrusted trout with a fork. The flesh fell apart in pale pink flakes. "All done," said Mom.

"NO!" I wailed.

"It's okay, dear," said Mom. "I heated up some spaghetti for you."

I could barely breathe. "*No! No! No!* That was my fish!"

They looked at me like I had four heads. "*Your* fish? You *hate* fish."

"But it was *my* fish! You should have ASKED. You went right ahead and COOKED it without even asking! YOU HAD NO RIGHT TO COOK MY TROUT!"

"FRANKIE!" Dad barked, a sound that could stop a train. "Enough! You will explain in a civil tone what the heck has gotten into you or get your butt to your room until you can!"

I slumped into a chair. "You've ruined everything."

"Frankie," Mom said softly. "*You* bought this trout?"

"Yes ... no ... I caught it."

"You went fishing?" Dad asked.

"Sort of."

"*Where* did you catch it?" he asked eagerly, but checked himself. "Hey, didn't I tell you it's only catch and release this time of year?"

"I got it at the U-fish."

"What U-fish?"

"Up behind the dairy."

"Wow, he sure grows some nice fish!"

Mom sighed. "I don't understand. Why on earth would you catch a fish, put it in the fridge and not say anything about it?"

"I found this bird and —"

"Oh, Frankie," Mom groaned, "not again. Those hopeless creatures always bring you down."

"It's *not* hopeless! It's going to fly away real soon. If it doesn't starve to death first — now that *you've* cooked its food. It can't eat cooked fish!"

"What bird eats trout?" Dad asked.

"It's a petrel. A Wilson's Storm-petrel. It just had a concussion. All it needed was a few days' rest and fish to eat. *That* fish!"

"How do you know it had a concussion?" said Mom. "Let your father have a look. Where is it?"

"In my closet."

Everyone paraded into my room. Even Bernie, who had shown up when the shouting began. She looked at the petrel and said, "Weird. What's that tube on top of its beak?" She didn't wait for an answer. "It smells fishy in here," she whined, and left.

At least Dad agreed with my diagnosis. "But it still seems like a lot of fish for one tiny bird."

"Not any more. It won't eat *cooked* fish! And it has to be fed in a few hours."

"I'd be happy to catch another one for you," said Dad.

"Bob. Anniversary party?"

Dad sagged. "Oh, right."

Mom asked, "Why don't you get your new friend to help you?"

"My new friend?"

"Maura-Lee."

"Huh?" I sputtered. "Why her?"

"The U-fish. It belongs to her father."

"Her father?"

"Yeah. Mr. Chisholm. The garbage man."

CHAPTER 18

Maura-Lee's Father

The planet tilted sideways. "How can the garbage man be Maura-Lee's father?"

Dad looked at Mom in mock shock. "Didn't you tell him where babies come from?"

Mom's jaw dropped. "I thought *you* did!"

"Oh, wait, you're right," Dad said, peering at me. "I *did.* More than once."

"You're the perfect father," Mom crooned.

Dad puffed out his chest. "True, but it's a hard word to live up to."

My head reeled. My butt found my bed. It didn't make sense. If the garbage man was Maura-Lee's father, then the Rottweiler was Maura-Lee's dog. Why did Maura-Lee run from her own dog?

And her own father?

"It doesn't make sense."

"I remember when Maura-Lee was little," said Mom.

"She'd pretend he wasn't her father ..."

"That's sad," said Dad.

"But the really sad thing was ... he let her. Maybe nothing has changed."

I wondered what it would be like to have a father with half a face — a face that sent small children screaming, a face kids told horrible stories about.

"So he didn't ... um ... his whole family wasn't killed in a fire?"

"No," said Dad, running his hand softly up Mom's back. "He got burned saving Maura-Lee. He lost the house. Not long after, his wife left him. Poor buddy."

"Oh," was all I could say. No one said anything until Dad finally asked, "So does this thing fly?"

"Huh?"

"The bird."

"Not really ... but its wings are fine. It's just pretty cramped in here."

"So let's take it up to the hallway," said Dad.

"I'll shut Pookey in the bathroom," said Mom. "But this better not take too long. Supper's ready."

The upstairs front hall was twice the length of my bedroom. I carefully lifted the petrel. Its heart vibrated against my fingertips. I tossed. The bird spread its wings. Yes! This was it! It flew — like a dark paper airplane, wings stiff and still — down the hall, into the living room and crash landed under the coffee table.

"Hmm," said Dad. "Another try?"

"Frankie," said Mom. "The bird could have brain

damage. It might not be able to fly. Bob, you tell him."

"Your mother could be right, but I'd give it another day or two."

Mom sighed. "Supper. Now."

Dad smacked his lips and rubbed his palms together. "Got to go eat. Trout's getting cold."

I took my spaghetti and the petrel back to my room and chewed over the future. The petrel was going to fly. It had to. I needed it to. But even if it flew tomorrow evening, it would need three more meals.

I had to go back to the U-fish.

Mom was just finishing her makeup. "Oh, Frankie, perfect timing." She strutted like a runway model, paused, turned. "So what do you think?"

"That green matches your eyes." She liked that, and it was true. "I need some money."

"Didn't I lend you eight dollars yesterday?"

"Yeah, and you ate it tonight."

"Right. There's a ten in my purse."

I grabbed my board and crammed on my helmet. The sun had finally broken through and pumped heat into the evening. I sped down Brookland Street hill, carved onto College Street and across the big bridge. I decided against the tree path. I'd go straight up the driveway and pray the dog was chained. I ollied the tracks and cruised the dairy's parking lot, pushing around the blind turn and past a gravel road that ran uphill to the neatly mowed grass and towering trees of a graveyard. Deep-throated sheep baaed from a farm beyond.

Around another tight turn a tall, hand-painted sign read "Chisholm's U-fish." An arm-long wooden trout pointed to a narrow uphill driveway crowded on either side by spruce forest.

I popped my board and marched up the driveway, hoping my brain would believe my confident strides, like the way smiling can trick your brain into thinking you're happy. As the road crested the slope, it split. The right fork led to the trailer. The brown garbage truck stood out front, its hood half swallowing someone in green coveralls. A booming woof shook the air.

"Shut up, you stupid dog!" the voice under the hood barked back.

The Rottweiler stiff-legged out from behind the truck, lowered his head at me and repeated, "Baa-roof!"

"How many times do I have to tell you to shut up?" Mr. Chisholm jumped down, a long wrench in his fist, like he was about to adjust the dog's behavior right there. Then he saw me. "Oh, sorry," he said. Not to me.

He brushed away a fly, leaving a streak of grease across his unscarred cheek. "How's the petrel?"

"Um ... pretty good," I stammered, keeping my eyes on the dog. "Um, I need another trout."

The man rubbed the dog's ears. "Another?"

"Um, yeah. Maura-Lee caught one for me on Tuesday."

Mr. Chisholm focused sharply on me. At least his one good eye did.

"I paid her for it!"

Still he stared, his half-missing face making his expression unreadable.

"But tonight my mom found the fish in the fridge," I babbled, "and she cooked it. And the petrel won't eat cooked fish, and, well, you know that ... so I need another one ... a small one is okay ... I'm letting the bird go tomorrow ..."

"How do you know my daughter?"

"Ah ... she's in my class."

He kept staring.

"And ... we both do that rehabilitative riding thing ... I mean, we're not the riders .... we walk ... well, actually, I *did* ride Prince ... twice ... but I was just helping Joey ..."

"So can *you* tell me what upset Maura-Lee last night?"

I shook my head. "Sorry."

"Are you sure?" He sounded desperate.

"I thought things went well last night."

The big man's shoulders drooped. "Ever since she got that horse she comes home one day saying the world is perfect and the next she's so miserable she won't get out of bed." He sighed through his teeth, a sound like a bicycle tire with a fast leak. "Keeping that horse was a *big* mistake."

The trailer door exploded open. "PRINCE WAS NOT A BIG MISTAKE!" Maura-Lee stood on the steps, eyes red, fists clenched.

The Rottweiler whined and wagged its bobbed tail.

Maura-Lee's father said tightly, "That horse is supposed to make you happy."

"Prince makes me happy!"

"Last night was happy? Today is happy? I think we should sell him."

"Mom bought him for *me*. He's *MY* horse!"

"And who got stuck paying for board and lessons and all that stuff he needs? Half the time you don't even like the horse!"

"I *love* Prince! If you sell him I will *hate* you! I will *hate* you *forever!*" She stormed down the driveway.

"Little Birdie ..." He reached for her arm as she passed, but she dodged and kept walking.

His tone tightened again. "Where are you going? Your friend needs a trout."

Maura-Lee spun around and glared. "He's not my friend." But she marched down to the shed, grabbed a net and a handful of food pellets, threw the pellets at the pond and jabbed in the net. Then she marched back up and flung the net at my feet, flopping fish and all. "Here!" She stomped down the driveway, muttering, "Stupid, stupid, stupid, stupid."

Her father stopped the fish's struggle with his wrench. "I'll get you a bag," he said quietly and disappeared into the trailer. Things bumped and banged and banged and bumped. Finally he returned with a bag.

I thought to say thank you but my lips wouldn't move. I pulled the ten dollars out of my pocket.

He shook his head and sat down heavily on the truck bumper. "She already hates me." He was talking to himself. At least I hoped he was talking to himself. I backed away.

The huge dog whined and stared past me down the driveway. I followed its gaze. That's when I saw the tree — a massive elm, like a preacher reaching his arms to the heavens, so tall the other trees seemed to kneel around it. At its base a blackened chimney held up the remains of a burned-out house. Behind me light streamed through sunset clouds, painting the scene a soft orange.

Orange.

The sirens and screams, the house swelling with fire, the little girl ... with the melted arms. I stumbled down the driveway unable to breathe, suffocated by my orange dream. It was real. The little girl was Maura-Lee.

CHAPTER 19

The Graveyard

I thought I was going to puke.

Maura-Lee's house burned and Maura-Lee burned and her father burned and her mother left and ... and it was *all my fault.* I dreamed the fire. I *knew* it was going to happen. And I didn't stop it. It was *all my fault!*

The wind slapped my face. NO! It wasn't my fault! Don't be so *stupid!*

But you dreamed it.

How was I supposed to know what it meant?

You dreamed the tree and the house. Right there in that very same spot.

I was five years old! *No one* listens to five-year-olds!

You didn't even try!

But maybe it wasn't a future-dream. Maybe it happened that night — like the petrel's accident. I probably heard the fire trucks in my sleep. Or I saw it on TV the next day, or a picture in the newspaper. *Then* I dreamed about it. It was an ordinary nightmare! Perfectly normal!

I took a deep breath. Of course. That was me. Normal. It wasn't my fault.

A blue jay screamed from the depths of the spruce beside me. I jumped and broke into a shaky jog down to the main road. As I dropped my skateboard on the pavement I heard huffing behind me. I stiffened and turned slowly. The Rottweiler stood there, his enormous pink tongue slung out the side of his enormous white-toothed jaws.

Then the dog lowered his head and whined. Then he sniffed the ground, walked by me and stood facing town. I got on my board and pushed off carefully, rolling wide to the other side of the road, slow and easy, praying the beast would ignore me and go back home. He didn't. He trotted on ahead, not letting me pass, occasionally looking over his shoulder as if to make sure I was still there.

If I lagged behind he slowed down and began whining again. Around the curve, he walked up the gravel road to the graveyard. Maura-Lee must have gone up there. He turned and woofed softly, more a cough than a bark. He looked from me to the hill and back.

Something is wrong.

"What do you want from me? It's not my fault she's screwed up."

That's when I remembered Bernie asking if she was suicidal. I didn't know the answer. And suddenly I knew I couldn't make the same mistake twice. I couldn't walk away again.

The sun's last rays lit the tips of the trees. There was maybe a half hour of skylight left. I had no desire to be in a graveyard after dark.

Small, unripe crab apples covered the gravel like ball bearings, threatening to roll me off my feet. Higher up, the hill flattened and stretched back in uneven rows of headstones — tall sandstone columns, wide black granites, dull white slabs and plain wooden crosses.

Three ancient chestnut trees shaded the crest of the hill. Maura-Lee hunkered against the smallest tree. The Rottweiler walked over and lay down beside her with a loud groan.

"Saber!" Maura-Lee snapped. "What are you doing here? You know you're not allowed off the property by yourself. Bad dog! You could have been hit by a car!"

"It's okay," I said. "He's with me."

She flinched. "Go away!" The dairy machinery across the road below us thrummed. She hugged her knees, rubbing her hands along her forearms where her long sleeves hid the scars I knew were there. The scars that weren't my fault.

A breeze pushed little leaves out of the trees. No, not leaves — birds. Dark gray on top, white below. Half-and-halfs, Patsy had called them the day Cannon asked the class what kinds of birds we knew. He had said they were juncos.

A little half-and-half landed on the gravestone nearest me. Its tiny claws gripped the gray-green lichen that roughed up the white marble. *1859–1941 ... His memory lives on.*

Maura-Lee ripped out a handful of grass and threw it as hard as she could. It fell gently to earth. "My father *never* understands!" she growled.

The soft orange sky reflected off a polished gray granite stone to my left. *DIED 1888. To angel form thy spirit grown. Thy God has claimed thee for his own.*

"Prince DOES make me happy!"

1879–1933 ... He leadeth me beside the still waters.

"I do *everything* Vanessa taught me, but he ignores me. I can't get it right. I'll never get it right!"

"It looked pretty amazing on Monday. It looked like dancing."

"But last night he walked away! I couldn't stop him. I'm so stupid!"

"Does he do that a lot?"

"NO ... See? See how stupid I am? I KNOW it was just one little thing, but I can't stop thinking about it — over and over and over. Then everything goes black." She pressed the heels of her hands against her skull. "Black, black, BLACK! Like there's this huge storm in my brain. And I can't stop it ... and I ..." She gasped up a sob. Then another.

I placed my helmet and the fish on my board, kicked away two round, spiny chestnut pods and sat down next to a flat reddish stone. *Age 13 years 11 months. And a small child shall lead them.*

"I hate myself."

"But you're the smartest, most talented person I know."

"So why can't I stop hating myself?"

I chewed my lower lip for a bit. "You're not ...?"

"What?"

"Well, you're in a graveyard and ..."

"Thinking of killing myself?"

I nodded.

"No."

It felt like one of those big gravestones just got hauled off my shoulders.

Then she said, "Sometimes."

The stone pressed down again. "But ..." I had nothing. Why did I come up here? I had a normal home, normal family. How could I know what to say to someone like Maura-Lee?

"What about Prince?" I blurted. "If you weren't here, who would look after him?"

Maura-Lee dried her face with her sleeve. "You're right. I would *never* leave Prince."

"So, why the graveyard?"

"It's quiet."

The dairy's thrumming, the trill of crickets, the sheep's deep bleats, a tractor chugging a bale of hay across the neighboring field. "Um, no, it isn't."

"Not outside." She waved her hand at the graves. "*They* don't *feel* anymore. It's quiet" — she tapped her forehead — "up here."

"The color thing?" I tried to humor her. "See? There's *another* talent — a seriously cool one."

Maura-Lee flipped on me. "Well, you can have it! Do you think knowing what everyone is feeling is *fun?* Knowing when people are sad or scared and not being able to do anything about it? Not being able to change it? You have no idea what that's like!"

Like dreaming about a rider with a red jacket who hits

her head? Or your grandmother saying good-bye forever? Or a house engulfed in flames and flesh burning and —

"You're right. I don't."

I lay on my back. A strange calmness crept over me. Maura-Lee and I had something in common: really good imaginations.

The graveyard glowed softly — lit from thunderheads stacked up like scoops of orange-pineapple ice cream. Below, swirling layers of pink blended into gray.

"When I was a kid," I said, "I used to lie in the grass a lot and watch the clouds float by and wonder at the depth of the sky and how high a bird could fly ... and I don't know why I just said that."

"My Dad still treats me like a kid," she whined, but there was a hint of a smile in her voice.

"Mine, too."

"Have you always liked flying?"

"I guess. You horses?"

"Yup. Vanessa says it's often genetic."

"Your mom?"

"She *hates* horses."

"But she bought you Prince."

"Because she knows Dad can't afford to keep him."

I thought about that for a while, then said, "Tim works for Vanessa to help pay for lessons and board and stuff. Maybe —"

"I already do." She stood up. "I've got to get home."

We walked toward the main road. Saber calmly followed. Dusk flattened the shadows, hiding the bumps and ruts. We very carefully navigated the slope of scattered crab apples. A deep rumbling followed the thunderheads in the distance, and a sudden cold wind blew the crickets silent.

"How's the petrel doing?"

I thought to say, "Fine, it's going to fly away tomorrow," but heard myself tell the truth. "Its wings are okay, but when I try to get it to fly it just glides to the ground. Doesn't flap at all."

"Maybe it's afraid of hitting the ceiling. Why not take it outside?"

"What if it flies a little but not enough to go back to the ocean? If it gets too far away to find then it'll starve to death for sure."

"I know where the ceiling is really high and the bird can't get too far away."

"Where?"

"The indoor arena. You could go out early on Saturday. No one uses the arena until nine."

I sighed. "Too far. Dad works Saturday mornings and Mom hates to get up on weekends. And she's not exactly in favor of me rescuing birds."

"Dad drives me out at seven on Saturdays. I stay all day, but I could ask him to wait for you and take you back. He likes birds."

"The petrel might fly tomorrow."

She shrugged. "See ya."

I pushed for home, ollied the tracks and sped along College Street. The petrel *had* to fly tomorrow. No way I was going to be seen driving through town with the Man with Half a Face *and* Weird Maura-Lee.

CHAPTER 20

From Bad to Worse

The petrel couldn't go on eating trout and living in my closet forever. Mom wouldn't let it ... and my heart couldn't take it.

I tried praying again.

I don't mean "Please, God, let it fly," pretty-please pleading. No, I mean negotiation — what you get for what I get. Okay, you're not supposed to bargain with God, but that night I prayed my brains out.

"Please, God, if you make it fly, I'll be *really good.* I won't swear. I won't lie. I'll even be nice to Bernie. Hey, and, God, don't do it just for me — do it for the petrel. It *needs* to fly. It's come so far. It's just one life. One tiny little life. No big deal, right?"

And then I dreamed.

I was outside somewhere — low hummocks and shadows, tall waving reeds and quiet flowing water. Fingers of light poking through clouds. Everything red-gold. I bent down and tucked the petrel into a tall clump of red-gold grass and turned toward town. A shape in the bushes ... a fox, red-gold and silent, streaking toward the marsh. I ran back, lungs aching for air.

Too late.

I woke up, tears on my face. A color dream? NO. I was over that idea. Just a bad dream ... an ordinary nightmare. Still, it left me feeling useless, helpless and totally lousy.

Friday went from bad to worse.

The petrel couldn't fly, wouldn't try, whatever. Pleading and praying hadn't worked, so I stuck it back in the closet. The less I looked at it the better. It was not a day to fly anyway. Rain bounced so hard the strong wind barely shifted the downpour sideways and the kitchen radio announced rain until midnight.

Then my toast jammed and burned and I knocked my bowl of cereal on the floor trying to get to the toaster before the smoke alarm went off. I didn't make it. The ear-splitting scream woke up Bernie, who added her screams — it was *my* fault she forgot to set her alarm and *Dad's* fault she had four new zits (from pizza) and *Mom's* fault she had to spend an extra half-hour in the shower. So *I* couldn't get a shower and had to wash in the sink and hope I didn't stink. But I did because I couldn't find my sneakers and Mom had to leave without me and I had to run to school and I sweated so much it was wetter in my raincoat than outside.

At least I got to class before Maura-Lee, so she couldn't ask me about the petrel or mention last night. I made it to my seat, sweaty and smelly and sure the day had to improve ... until Mrs. Rose dropped a surprise test on us — a surprise to me because I had completely forgotten about it.

In English class Roddie asked a confused question and Bomb started in on him. First a funny comment, then a wisecrack, then double-edged sarcasm. The rest of the room laughed loudly and Roddie tried to smirk it off, but it was all I could do not to pop Bomb one to shut him up.

Then, for some bizarre reason, in math Mr. McKenna asked *me* question after question. Maybe he hoped I'd be able to answer one out of fifty, but that day I couldn't add two plus two.

Even the hallways were a nightmare. TGIF pumped up the volume, the energy and the jostling — and the rain penned it all indoors. Then there was Maura-Lee. She had a knack for appearing out of nowhere. I got an ache in my neck trying to look five ways at once. By history class I was exhausted, and I hit my head hard against the corner of the bookshelf when I dozed off.

Then at lunch Mike tortured Tim and me by practicing his speech for the provincial 4-H public-speaking competition. Okay, I admit the part about the cows in the kitchen was really funny, the single light in my dark, dark day. The afternoon was no better. When the last bell rang I bolted out the back door and stood against the south corner of the building, watching the townies stream off school property and waiting for a certain red jacket to disappear over Elm Street hill. Another downpour drummed on my raincoat hood. That's why I didn't hear Slug sneak up behind me. He nailed me with a vicious punch in my lower back.

"What was that for?" I bellowed. My only answer was Slug's dark laughter as he sloshed to his bus.

I swear my legs went numb for a full five minutes. I walked home slowly, not trusting my feet. It hurt to bend down and feed the petrel. The bird ate well but wouldn't fly. Then Mom cooked the dreaded leftovers for supper — unidentifiable and pretty well inedible. The Friday night concert at the gazebo in River Park was washed out and the TV had nothing but repeats. By nine, three pain pills got me semi-comfortable in the computer chair and I hooked up with Tim on-line, only to find the site flooded with five million other bored teenagers, and it locked up before we got near the fifth level.

Then Bernie yelled that the phone was for me and when I went to get it she hogged the computer for the rest of the night. The only good thing was that Bernie had answered the phone instead of Mom: it was Maura-Lee.

"You want that ride to Hug a Horse in the morning?"

How could I drive through town with Weird Maura-Lee and the Man with Half a Face? Risk the rest of my teenage years in Antigonish for the sake of a bird? Why hadn't I just left it in the schoolyard? Left it where the wind had dropped it. Where Paul would have put it out of its misery — and prevented mine.

"Yeah," I answered.

"Okay. We'll come by at 6:45."

"NO! I mean ... um ... I don't want to wake up Mom. I'll meet you at the bridge."

"Okay." She hung up.

I lay on my aching back, with one pillow under my knees and two under my head. I was still staring at the darkness long after Bernie shut down the computer and went up to her room. The house was so quiet I could hear the gurgle of the refrigerator upstairs. Whenever my eyes closed I shifted my position so pain would force me awake ... so I wouldn't go to sleep ... so tomorrow wouldn't come. Around 3:30 I remember praying, "Please let the bird fly ... don't let me ruin my life for nothing ... and don't let me dream ..."

CHAPTER 21

A Dream Come True

Next thing I knew my alarm squawked. Tomorrow had come. I fed the petrel less than usual, in case a full stomach made it too heavy for lift-off.

I took a record-breaking shower and I checked my back in the double mirror. A royal-blue bruise spread out from my spine like the tattoo of a nuclear explosion.

Since I was going to a barn, I grabbed the jeans from the not-too-stiff-with-mud-yet pile and my old black hoodie. Then I gently picked up the petrel. "You're going for a trip, little buddy. I'm going way out of my way for you so don't blow it, eh? *Today you fly!*"

It was hard to look it in the eye. My chest ached. I placed it back in the shoebox and put some tape on the cover for security.

I leaned on the bridge railing wishing I was holed up in a cave someplace. Sunlight skimmed along the heads of trees, highlighting their new reds and yellows. Below me, the royal-blue water rippled past. Two black ducks stood on small boulder islands busily rubbing their big bills all over their feathered bodies and quack-quacking softly. The air moseyed down the tracks from the east-end Tim Horton's, bringing the strong fragrance of coffee and fresh doughnuts. A single granola bar was not enough for breakfast.

A car drove across the bridge and turned up the golf course road. There was almost no traffic noise from town, and it struck me that at 6:40 on a Saturday morning no one my age would be awake. No one would see me with Maura-Lee and the Man with Half a Face. No one in town or at Hug a Horse.

Then I heard the grouching of a leaky muffler coming around the sharp turn. A rust-streaked silver Nissan pickup pulled up. The passenger door opened.

"Good morning," said Mr. Chisholm. "Scootch over, Maura-Lee. Give the boy room."

Maura-Lee narrowed on the bench seat, avoiding contact on both sides.

"Pass the box to Maura-Lee. You'll need two hands to slam that darn door."

I handed Maura-Lee the shoebox, climbed up and pulled the door shut with a loud thump. It promptly swung open.

"*Two* hands," said Maura-Lee.

I gritted my teeth and *slammed* the sucker. That worked.

"Did you fall?" Maura-Lee asked, looking at the dried mud on my knees.

"Not today," I mumbled. My face got hot. Maura-Lee

had on crisp denims, and her father wore a navy work shirt and pants, worn but clean as a whistle. The ancient truck was spotless, too — lemony-fresh from a very recent cleaning. I made a lame attempt to rub the mud off my knees with my cuff.

"Seatbelts," the garbage man ordered.

We buckled up and drove through town. College Street was still asleep — old family homes, the funeral parlor, apartments rented to students — all silent. Same with the stores on Main. There were two men on the sidewalk, but they were busy watering the gaudy flower baskets hung on every lamppost and store front. A few cars on Church Street, probably coming from the twenty-four-hour grocery, but the drivers didn't look over.

Between the noise of the truck (it had more rattles than it had parts), the sun in my eyes and no one talking, it was a surprisingly decent trip. As we turned onto the road to Meadow Green, we swung wide to avoid a pothole full of muddy water — three unmatched hubcaps hanging from neighboring shrubs warned it was a real wheel-eater. Around the next bend two more hubcaps had been propped against a telephone pole, waiting to return to their owners and telling drivers to slow down before the next series of frame-cracking moguls.

"The Department of Highways better grade this road soon. I'm sick of abusing my truck like this," Mr. Chisholm complained.

I looked over at him, at the pink putty side of his face. So many scars. Not my fault.

The sound of scrambling on cardboard startled me.

Maura-Lee had tipped up the box on her lap.

"You have to keep the bird level."

She passed the box to me. The petrel skittered more. "You should have put something in there for it to hold on to."

"I guess."

"So, Frankie, right? Is it going to fly today?" her father asked.

"Um ... yeah. At least I hope so." I *really* hoped so.

We approached the long straight stretch between pastures and fields of cut corn. Washboard ridges pounded us to a crawl. The truck suddenly swerved around something dark green on the road.

"Looks like half a mailbox," Maura-Lee said. "Someone wasn't watching where they were going."

"They knew exactly where they were going," her father said. "Some moron's idea of Friday-night fun." He pointed toward the next mailbox with its middle bashed so far in that the painted deer on the side kissed its white-tailed butt.

"There's another one." Blue and white, with the top ripped off. "And another." He shook his head. "What kind of idiot gets a kick out of destroying other people's property?"

I couldn't answer. I couldn't breathe. The last box was blue ... royal blue ... and crushed ... just like the mailbox in my dream. When was that? Wednesday night? Thursday, Friday, Saturday ... three days ago. Three days. Nanna died *three* days after the turquoise dream!

No! It's a coincidence. Mailboxes got smashed all the time.

Pay attention to coincidences.

Nanna, shut up!

Mr. Chisholm muttered, "It's been a long time since I've seen that stupid mailbox-bashing stunt."

Maura-Lee looked at me. "Something wrong?"

Why did she ask? Was I glowing green or purple or brown or ... what was the color of fear? "Nothing," I said. Absolutely nothing.

Vanessa was in the outdoor ring riding Belle ... or maybe Fleur. As we climbed out of the truck, she trotted up to the fence, halted and stroked the horse on the neck. The horse reached out her nose and yawned a huge white-toothed yawn right in my face. She had no bit in her mouth. How could Vanessa stop her without a bit?

"Good morning, John," Vanessa called. "Good morning, Maura-Lee. Frankie, what brings you out so early? Don't tell me you've caught the horse bug, too!"

"It was my idea," said Maura-Lee, all businesslike. "That petrel of his won't fly in the house so I thought maybe it would fly in the indoor arena. And if it can't, we can still catch it."

Vanessa smiled brightly. "Mind if I watch? Just give me a moment to turn Belle out and then I'll close the arena doors.

"I'll help with the doors," said the garbage man.

I sat on the worn wooden bench next to the ring with the shoebox on my lap. Maura-Lee stood a ways away watching me, and I don't mean simply looking. It gave me the creeps.

What color was she seeing now? Could I change it if I tried? If I thought really happy thoughts — the petrel's wonderful wings ... its jewel eyes ... the rustle of its dark feathers ... the browns, black when wet ... a wet lump of garbage ... the tall wet grass ... the red-gold fox ... I snapped back to the sunshine and the six horses grazing behind the house, my heart pounding.

Belle scampered across the hill to join her friends. She sidestepped into Prince's shoulder. He pinned his ears and snaked his head at her chest. When she didn't move, he pulled back his lips and punched her in the butt with his huge teeth. Maura-Lee laughed. Belle hopped forward and the whole herd bounced a few strides then settled down with noses in the grass.

The arena doors rumbled closed. Vanessa shouted, "All ready, people."

We all stood at one end of the arena. I carefully peeled the tape off the box lid and opened it. The petrel sat up. It looked around, cocking its head in little robotic movements, this way and that. It looked interested in the big space.

"Okay, little fellow," I said quietly. "Here's your chance." I slipped my hands under the bird, feeling its vibrating heart nearly matching my own — please fly, please fly, please fly.

Maura-Lee whispered, "Come on, little bird. You can do it!"

I held the petrel out at arm's length. It stood up in my hands. I felt its tiny weight shift left, right, left. I took a deep breath and threw my hands up. The little bird spread its wings wide, so wide ... and glided ... glided ... and landed halfway down the arena.

My heart landed in my feet.

"Let's try again," Vanessa said softly.

"What's the point," I said. But I did. The result was the same.

"Well, that's too bad," Mr. Chisholm said.

Vanessa tried to cheer me up: "maybe it was meant to be," "you tried your best," "these things happen." All I heard was "you failed, you failed, you failed." And what about the petrel? What was I supposed to do with it now? I put it in the box and pressed the tape back in place.

Mr. Chisholm looked at his watch. "I've got to get going. I'll be back at four-thirty, okay, Maura-Lee?"

"Make that five-thirty," Vanessa said.

"Okay," he said. "Better get your lunch from the truck. Frankie, I'll drop you at home."

We bumped back through Meadow Green, past the crumbled royal-blue mailbox. A high-pitched engine screamed behind us. A four-wheeler pulled alongside. The driver flashed a wild grin and gunned it up the road.

Slug!

"What kind of parent lets their kid drive without a helmet?" the garbage man ranted. "It's dangerous *and* against the law!"

That's when I saw the hoof prints in the soft dirt. All my blood drained out of me. A horse on the road ... and a four-wheeler ... and that mailbox —

"There's going to be an accident!" I squeaked.

"At some point."

"No. NOW! Up ahead. There's a horse on the road. There's going to be an accident. *We have to stop it!*"

Mr. Chisholm frowned with the good side of his mouth. I don't know if it was the terror on my face or the reckless way Slug was sliding sideways out of sight around the next turn, but the man said, "Maybe I better keep an eye on that idiot," and stepped on the accelerator. The truck rushed forward, battling the rough road.

The idiot came into view. So did a small blond girl on a big, speckled white pony — Kim on Jelly Bean. And a car, a rusty old Ford Focus, rolling slowly down the dead center of the road.

Slug revved his engine, fishtailing up the shoulder, spewing a rooster-tail of gravel at Jelly Bean. The pony threw her head up and skittered sideways. Kim hauled her back. Any second the car would pull over. Any second now.

It kept coming.

"What the —?" Mr. Chisholm dropped his foot off the accelerator. The old engine stalled ... and backfired. *Bang! Bang!* Jelly Bean leaped forward. She hit the car head on. Her front legs lifted. Her wide belly landed on the front hood. The windshield fractured. The bumper skidded Jelly Bean's hind legs backward along the gravel at least a car length before the vehicle finally stopped.

The screaming began — a fire alarm of a scream.

Mr. Chisholm jumped out and ran to the car. The petrel scratched in its box. I had forgotten I was holding it. I placed it carefully on the seat, got out and closed the truck door. It swung back open, the big side mirror sweeping past, revealing a look of misery and fear all mashed into one ... just like in my dream. But it wasn't on Slug's face. It was on *mine.*

And just like in my dream, the screaming continued, filling up Meadow Green. It came from the girl in the driver's seat. Haley, from Tim's class, a leggy redhead who wore too much makeup and acted way older than was good for her. A blond boy in a black-and-gold high school jacket was yelling at her, "Put your foot on the brake! Put your foot on the brake!"

Kim was standing on the roof of the car still holding the loop of Jelly Bean's reins. Later she said she had simply stepped off the pony as easily as getting out of a chair. Jelly Bean thudded her knees on the hood, desperate to get her front feet under her. She slid off over the fender and landed heavily on her side with a grunt. Kim tobogganed down the rear window and over the trunk as Jelly Bean lurched to her feet, bright red blood dripping from her mouth. Mr. Chisholm helped them to the side of the road.

He turned to the car, leaned over the driver's window and said to Haley in a strong, fatherly tone,

"Calm down. Calm down."

Haley looked at the Man with Half a Face and her screaming cranked up another whole octave.

Mr. Chisholm bellowed, "BE QUIET!"

All sound stopped except for the crickets. Down by the river, a white-faced cow mooed at its half-grown calf.

Kim stroked Jelly Bean's face and cooed softly, "It's okay, girl. It's okay, girl,"

"Are you all right?" Mr. Chisholm asked Haley. She nodded.

"What happened? Why did you drive into the horse?"

"I didn't ..." Haley said weakly. She looked at the boy. "Donnie?"

Donnie jumped out of the car. His pale eyebrows crammed into a single angry line. "That crazy horse ran into *us!* Look at my car! It smashed my damn car!" His mouth grew larger by the second. "Someone's going to pay for this! What's your name?" he shouted at Kim. "What's your father's name?"

Kim's eyes widened briefly, then her face hardened. She squared her shoulders and spoke as if she was a head taller than Donnie. "*You* were on *my* side of the road."

"*Your* side of the road? You shouldn't be *on* a road! That nag was totally out of control!"

"No, she wasn't!" Kim bit out each word with astounding control. "The creep on the four-wheeler hit her with rocks. All things considered, she was *really, really* good! If y*ou,*" she glared at Haley, "had stayed on *your* side of the road, everything would have been fine."

"YOU HIT US!"

"NO, I DIDN'T!"

Mr. Chisholm said, "It looked to me like you two ran into each other."

"*Your* car's on the wrong side of the road!" Kim exclaimed, pointing at the dented Ford.

"*Your* horse forced us over here!" Donnie hollered.

A tiny hint of fear flushed across Kim's face. She looked at me. "Frankie, you saw it. They were on *my* side of the road, right?"

I *did* see it. *Twice.* It wasn't Kim's fault. Or Haley's. Or even Slug's. It was *mine.*

CHAPTER 22

Muddy

I saw it in my dream. I *should* have stopped it.

"Frankie?" Kim repeated, a hint of tremble in her chin.

The car had been in the middle of the road. Both times. "They were over the center line," I muttered.

"There's no center line on a dirt road!" Donnie spewed. "And there was still plenty of room for that beast to go by. *She* ran into *us!*"

Kim turned to Mr. Chisholm. He shrugged his big shoulders. "Not sure."

Kim shrank to her original shortness. She shifted her feet back and forth and looked around as if help hid in the bushes lining the ditch. Her worry was my fault. The car with the broken windshield and dented hood ... my fault. The boy with the clenched fists, the driver holding herself with worry ... all my fault.

Suddenly a small thought popped up. *The driver.* Huh?

Haley was driving!

"Hang on," I said. "What the heck is *Haley* doing driving on a public road?"

"Where else is she going to drive?" Donnie snapped.

"You know this girl?" Mr. Chisholm asked me.

"She's in my grade."

The man peered at Haley. "Do you have a beginner's license?"

"I ... um," Haley flicked her long red hair off her shoulder and tipped her green eyes at Donnie.

Donnie didn't say anything.

"She can't," I said. "She's only fourteen."

Mr. Chisholm crossed his arms over his chest, the fingers of his gloved hand thrumming his bulky bicep. Donnie stormed around the car and jerked open the driver's door. "Move over," he ordered. He got in, gunned the old engine to life and drove off.

Mr. Chisholm shook his head and sighed through his teeth like air brakes released. "How's the horse?"

Jelly Bean licked foamy, pink saliva. The bleeding had stopped. Kim lifted the pony's upper lip. "She broke off half of one front tooth." She led the muddied pony around in a circle the width of the road. Jelly Bean followed with no obvious limp. When they stopped, the pony snuggled her broad head into Kim's chest. "She doesn't seem to be hurt," said Kim.

I saw the shaking start in Kim's knees. It climbed quickly. She grabbed the saddle as she burst into tears.

Mr. Chisholm pushed his hands into his pockets. "Now, now. Everything's okay. No one got hurt."

After a minute, Kim sucked in a last sob and wiped her face on her sleeve. The tears stopped. The trembling didn't.

"Maybe you better lead your horse home in case that idiot on the four-wheeler comes back," Mr. Chisholm said.

Kim nodded.

"Okay, then. Let's go, Frankie."

I realized then that there was a very good chance Slug might come back. He had found a way to get revenge on Kim. "I think I should stay with them."

"Of course. Good idea. I'll drop the bird off at your house."

"Thanks. Can you ask my mom to put it in the box in my closet?"

I followed Jelly Bean and Kim back along the road.

You dreamed the future!

It was not my imagination. All my life wanting to be special. *All* my life dreaming the future. A future I could do nothing about.

Look what happened when I tried. *I* got Mr. Chisholm to speed up. *Then* the truck backfired and scared Jelly Bean onto the car. I didn't *change* the future. I *created* it!

I dreamed it and it happened. What a freaking useless talent.

We approached Kim's big white house with its football field of a lawn out front and rusty, red barn behind.

"Jelly Bean is Tim's pony. I think I should take her up to his place and have him check her over, okay?"

"Sure."

A GMC pickup rattled toward us. Kim led Jelly Bean to the edge of the ditch and stood between her and the oncoming vehicle, stroking the pony's neck and crooning, "Easy girl, easy."

I backed away, my heart pounding. Vehicles were the new enemy; Jelly Bean could jump or run in any direction.

The truck slowed politely. Jelly Bean never even twitched. She just snatched the tops off some tall grass in the ditch, then pulled against the reins as if to say, let's get going.

"I thought she'd be scared," I said.

"Me, too," Kim replied.

We didn't talk anymore. The sun woke up a stiff south breeze and a flock of faded green leaves spiraled onto the road around us. We walked by wide flat yellow fields, up the grade between the evergreens and white birch and out into smaller fields backed by dark green hills. By the time we reached Tim's, the soft pad of hooves on dirt, the steady pitch of crickets and the lack of traffic had calmed my nerves.

Tim answered his door dressed only in jeans. "What are *you* doing here?" he asked, scratching his frizzy bedhead and yawning.

Kim let me deliver what was likely going to be Tim's favorite story for a very long time. A bird that wouldn't fly. A horse running over a car. Hard to beat. I left out Maura-Lee and her father (if she didn't want anyone to know who her father was it wasn't my business) and the fact that I knew what was going to happen before it did.

"Lord lifting lighthouses!" Tim shoved naked feet into sneakers and shuffled out to check Jelly Bean. He touched her gently all over, sing-saying silly things: Jellybelly, Missy-messy, Girlie-girl. "Except for the mud, she looks fine to me. I don't see any lumps or bumps, but something might swell up later. Let's take her up to Hug a Horse and get Vanessa's opinion." He dashed inside for a pair of socks, a crumpled purple T-shirt and a bagel that dripped honey down his wrist.

"So what kind of bird did you say you found?" Tim asked as we walked. "It's too late in the year for babies, isn't it?"

"Yeah. It's an adult. A Wilson's Storm-petrel. It must have hit its head in the storm last weekend. But it got over that."

"Where is it now?"

"Home. I stayed with Kim in case Slug came back for seconds."

"When's she picking you up?"

"Huh?"

"Your mom."

"Huh?"

"Your mo-ther. Mrs. Uc-cel-lo. The person who drove you here."

"Oh ... um ..." Before I could think of a good answer, Kim said, "The garbage man drove him out."

"The what?"

"You know. The guy ..." Kim placed her hand over one side of her face.

"Old Half-face?"

"His name is Mr. Chisholm," I said. "I've been getting trout from him to feed the petrel. He owns a U-fish. He likes birds, too."

"A U-fish? And he drove you out?"

I nodded as Tim tacked more juicy details onto his story.

"So the bird didn't fly, eh?"

"No."

"Sorry. What are you going to do with it now?"

"I don't know." And I didn't. All I knew was my dreams came true and on Sunday, three days after the red-gold dream, the petrel would be gone.

Tim suddenly stopped like he'd hit an invisible force field. "Holy heifers," he gasped. "I just remembered! *Happy birthday, Frankie!*"

I'd completely forgotten my own birthday.

"You know, your being here is pretty cool," Tim said. "Now I don't have to wait until suppertime to give you your present. Not that I was *actually* going to give it to you then ... not the *actual* present ..." The old goldfish-eaten grin plastered his face.

Tim yakked all the way to Hug a Horse Farm. It was pretty amazing — everything from soup to nuts, literally. Chicken noodle, homemade — Tim's favorite. And hazelnuts — how to pick them without getting all those nasty prickles in your fingers and how to dry them under the hay until the nut meats fall out. And, of course, horses. Every muzzle-kissing, mud-scraping, tack-oiling detail. I couldn't have gotten a word in edgewise if I'd tried.

But I didn't. I didn't want to talk. Or think. Or be me — the former Ace of Average, now Future-dreamer. And still totally useless.

Tim paused for breath when the rainbow fence came into sight. Maura-Lee was in the riding ring, jogging in a circle as Prince ran a bigger circle around her. When she saw us, she stopped and walked to the fence, an odd frown on her face.

Prince squealed a high-pitched greeting. Jelly Bean nickered back in a husky, unfeminine voice.

"Is this Jelly Bean?" Maura-Lee asked.

Tim filled with pride. "Sure is."

Vanessa, apple-picker in hand, stepped out of the barn to see what was up. "Good morning," she said, a puzzled crinkle in her brow. "Frankie, what are you doing back here?"

Tim launched like fireworks. *His* story lit the morning with drama and pizzazz.

"Frankie, it was sweet of you to stay with Kim," said Vanessa. "That boy you call Slug sounds like a menace." Then she spoke gently to the speckled pony and carefully checked her from toes to teeth.

Tim smoothed the feathery lock of hair between his pony's ears. She pushed her head toward him and tried to rub her face against his shoulder, but he stepped back. "Mind your manners, Missy."

Kim laughed. "She missed you."

"Yeah, missed trying to *own* me. You don't let her rub on you like that, do you?"

"She doesn't try."

"So how is she?" Tim asked Vanessa.

"She has a small chunk out of her left hind heel bulb and her knees are a bit puffy, but it shouldn't amount to much as long as she stays outside and keeps moving. Then there's that broken upper incisor. Horse teeth generally grow until they're around twenty. J.B.'s only twelve, so that tooth will eventually grow in. The main problem will be the bottom tooth opposite the broken one — it won't have anything to wear against. We'll have to file it even with the others now and then. Not a big deal."

"So she's okay?"

Vanessa thought for a long moment, lips pressed in a tight line. "I think so. But I'd really like to have Dr. Jane look at her to be sure. It's not every day a horse runs over a car!"

Tim sighed. "A farm call costs a lot of money."

"I've been planning on getting Puzzle's teeth checked," said Vanessa, "so that'll cover the farm fee, okay?"

"Okay."

"Right," said Vanessa. "Put her in her old stall for now. We'll turn her out in the ring when the girls finish their lesson. Kim, want to fetch her some apple treats from the orchard?"

At the word "treats," Jelly Bean jerked up her head and a sub-woofer wuffle fluttered her nostrils.

Tim chuckled. "Come on, Miss Piggy." He and Jelly Bean trailed Vanessa to the barn.

Prince followed Jelly Bean as far as the riding-ring gate. He pushed the gate with his head. When it didn't open he struck it with a front foot.

"Hold on," Maura-Lee ordered. Then she said to me, "What's eating you?"

"Me?"

"Yes, you. You're all *muddy.*"

I looked down at my jeans.

She let out an exasperated breath. "Not your clothes."

"Oh ... nothing," I lied.

Maura-Lee rolled her eyes and shook her head. She turned to her horse, now whomping the gate repeatedly. "*Men!*" she grumbled.

As she haltered Prince, the Freestar arrived. Lana jumped out. "I told you it was Prince's!" she shouted. "I win!"

Michelle argued, "No way. I know piles of pony poop when I see them."

"Maura-Lee," Lana said, "we saw fresh manure on the road. I bet it belonged to Prince. Michelle says it doesn't. You went for a ride this morning, right?"

Before Maura-Lee could answer, Prince dragged her toward the barn doorway that had swallowed Jelly Bean. He squealed so loud, Maura-Lee cringed. She jerked the lead rope. "Cut it out, you stupid horse!" Then she snapped at Lana, "It was Jelly Bean."

Margaret climbed out of the van. "Told you," she said, her freckles bunching into a grin.

"Frankie, what are you doing here?" Michelle asked. "Don't tell me you've been bitten by the bug!"

"Great!" Margaret crowed. "We could use some more boys around. Especially at haying time." She shoved up her sleeves, flexed her girly biceps and laughed.

"Welcome to the club, Frankie," said Lana. "Are you going to ride today?"

"No!"

"Then what *are* you doing here?"

"Right now I'm looking for a ride home."

"Oh, rats," said Michelle, smiling her pretty smile.

"And before?" Lana pried.

"Ask Tim."

Lana's eyes lit up. "Tim's here?" Then she shouted to her mother, who had gone to the orchard, "Mom, will you drive Frankie back to town?"

Her mother held a plastic grocery bag already bulging with yellow-green apples. "As soon as I fill this. Climb aboard, Frankie."

"HEY!" Tim hurried out of the barn. "Hey, man. You can't go home now. I haven't given you your birthday present."

"Is today your birthday?" Michelle asked. She, Lana and Margaret spontaneously broke into a horrible "Happy Birthday" harmony that ended in a mess of giggles. Lana's mother slid open the van door and thumped in the bag of apples. "That was truly awful."

"So right!" said Lana, laughing harder.

"Come on," Tim pleaded with me. "Stay. We'll have fun."

"Mom will be back at three," said Lana.

"I can't. I've got to get home and feed the petrel."

"The what-trel?" asked Michelle.

"Tim can tell you that, too."

Tim shook his head, but didn't argue. "Okay, I'll see

you at supper. Your present is scheduled for tomorrow anyway."

Margaret giggled and Michelle elbowed her to be quiet. I should have got the hint, but I didn't. Maura-Lee was right. My brain was mud.

Lana's mother was nice and didn't make me talk on the way home. "Hope you have a good birthday," was all she said as she dropped me off.

The house was quiet. Bernie's door was closed and there was a note on the fridge: *Frankie — bird back — gone for groceries — Happy Birthday! XOX!*

The trip to Hug a Horse must have given the petrel a huge appetite. Its neck bulged right down to its breast bone before it stopped snatching and gulping. Then it walked to the far end of the box, squirted a black-and-white poop, walked back, fluffed its dark feathers and sat down. It watched me watching it.

Why did I pick it up, force it to live in a cardboard box, prolong its life? Its suffering?

It looks fine.

That was the problem. It *looked* fine.

"What was the point of dreaming you, little bird? What am I going to do with you now?"

Sitting on the floor against my closet door, I cried like a little kid. I cried for the petrel, for the doomed birds before it, for Nanna, for Maura-Lee's scars, for Jelly Bean's swollen knees. All my pain, all my frustration, until the edge of the door ached my bruised back and nothing was left inside but an echo.

Then I did the only thing I could do. I went skateboarding. Hard and fast. I lost track of time. At some point a south wind barreled in on the edge of a dark squall line, solid as a wall. It arched across the sky, summer on one side, fall on the other. It sucked up leaves and dirt and litter, then spit it all in my face. I didn't care. I squinted against the flying grit and used the wind's power to push me faster than I had ever dared go. So the afternoon blew by.

Finally the wind relaxed and my missed lunch slowed me down. Thoughts of birthday cake called my stomach home.

"Having fun on your special day?"

"Yup."

"Did the little bird fly?"

"Nope."

"What are you going to do with it?"

"Give it back."

Mom nodded. "You better get cleaned up before your company comes."

"It's just Tim."

"Not exactly." She smiled brightly. Too brightly. "When Mr. Chisholm dropped the bird off, I invited Maura-Lee, too."

Chapter 23

Happy Birthday

"You WHAT! Well, you can un-invite her."

"I thought you two were friends."

"I can't be friends with her. She's weird."

"That's not nice!"

The doorbell rang. Mom put her hands on her hips. "That will be for you."

It had to be Maura-Lee. Tim didn't ring the bell. He walked in the back door and stuck his head in the fridge before even saying hello.

"I'm not answering it."

"Frankie, dear, I'm sorry, but I thought she was your friend, and when I asked Mr. Chisholm if Maura-Lee might like to come to your birthday supper, he said no one had ever asked her to a birthday party before. Can you believe it? That's just awful. So I said she just had to come. What can it hurt? Now go let her in. And *be nice.*"

"Happy birthday," Maura-Lee said softly, as I opened the door. She handed me a sparkly turquoise gift bag, then pressed her palms on her deep brown velvet skirt, holding it against the wind. The brown looked good with her pale green blouse and sky-blue sweater.

"Thanks." I had to look up slightly. In high heels, she was taller than me.

Mom bustled out of the kitchen. "Supper will be here any minute, unless your father's late. Frankie, go get changed into something nice, like Maura-Lee here. I'll give her a tour of the garden. Do you like flowers, dear?" she asked Maura-Lee. "Frankie's father is an excellent gardener."

Bernie trotted downstairs. "Hi," she said to Maura-Lee. "Nice shirt." I could see her looking at Maura-Lee's wrists, but over-long sleeves covered the scars. "I used to have one just like that but I gave it to the Opportunity Shop."

"Maybe it's the same one."

Bernie's eyes widened and her mouth clamped shut.

I had to smile. Not many people got the better of Bernie in less than twenty seconds.

"Well, I hope you can sing 'Happy Birthday' better than Tim," Bernie said, as she flounced away.

"I can sing," Maura-Lee assured her.

Maura-Lee sat on the two-seater swing. Crossed arms held her sweater tight as her bare legs pumped the swing in a high arc. The wind forced the arc sideways slightly, and the supporting chains twisted and clunked on every backstroke.

"Where is everyone?" she asked, dragging her heels to a stop.

"Tim's not here yet."

She looked confused. "It's not a party?"

"Nah, I haven't had a party since I was eight or nine. It's just my family and Tim ... and you."

"Oh." Sitting there in her fancy skirt and heels, the girl who could wear anybody's clothes and anybody's personality suddenly seemed lost.

"But there's going to be four kinds of pizza," I said, "because I couldn't make up my mind which kind I like best, and Mom loves having leftovers. And there's root beer. And a *huge* chocolate-peanut-butter cake — my great-grandmother's recipe. Mom always bakes one for birthdays. It's awesome. You're not allergic to peanuts are you?" I was babbling. Why was I babbling?

Maura-Lee shook her head.

The wind rattled the poplar like pebbles in a pop can.

"Nice swing," she said.

"Dad made it."

"Must have taken him a long time to cut every slat like that."

"Nah, he used old hockey sticks."

She nodded.

Silence.

"The wind's getting worse," I babbled some more. "The backside of another hurricane. They said it's going to sweep past Sable Island and blast

Newfoundland. I hope it lets off so I can release the petrel tomorrow."

"Why don't you keep it longer?"

"It has to go tomorrow."

"Did you dream that?"

"Yeah."

"Did it fly?"

"No. I left it in the grass. And there was a fox."

"It doesn't have to be like that. Now that you know, you can change it."

I shook my head. "The last time I only made the dream come true."

She was about to argue when Mom trotted down the deck steps. "Frankie, Tim just called. I'm afraid he's not coming. He's still up at Hug a Horse Farm." The pinch in her voice said much more.

"What's wrong?"

"There's a problem with his pony."

My mouth went dry. "A problem?"

She took a deep breath. "He said the vet was just out. Jelly Bean is blind."

Blind?

"I'm sorry. He said not to tell you until after supper — so as not to spoil your birthday — but I felt you needed to know. He sounded pretty upset. Maybe you should phone him when he gets home."

Blind!

Dad's bike rumbled into the garage. "Come on up in a few minutes," Mom said gently, and went to meet the pizzas.

Jelly Bean is blind! Tim's Jelly-belly, his most favorite thing in the whole entire universe — that he'd loved since he was six years old — is blind.

You made Jelly Bean blind!

Maura-Lee said quietly, "Now I know what that shade of blue means."

"Huh?"

"Jelly Bean was blue. I've never seen a horse blue like that."

"Me neither." I didn't mean to say it out loud.

Maura-Lee squinted at me. "You dreamed that, too, didn't you?"

A pit of misery opened at my feet. I fell in. "I thought it was just a ridiculous dream," I moaned. "So I ignored it. And I ignored the blue mailbox and then ... A blue horse, for Pete's sake! How was I supposed to know what to do? I couldn't stop you from hitting your head. Or Nanna from dying. Or the fire. I can't change the future. I can't do anything!"

"What fire?" Maura-Lee asked. Her face had turned to steel. "You dreamed about my house?"

I nodded helplessly — uselessly.

"*When?*"

"The night before my fifth birthday." It hurt to speak.

"*Nine* years ago?"

"I told *everyone*. They didn't listen."

Maura-Lee jumped to her feet. The swing banged against its chains. Her voice banged against my chest. "You dreamed about my house burning down *before* it happened! And you didn't stop it! *I lost everything! I lost EVERYTHING because of YOU!"* Her hands curled into white fists. She was going to punch me.

I deserved to be punched.

Mom called from the kitchen. "Come and get it."

We didn't move.

"Where are you two?" Mom trotted down the steps. And just like that, Maura-Lee straightened and smiled and followed Mom into the house.

I crawled out of my pit and dragged myself to the dining room.

"Hey there, birthday boy!" said Dad. "Sorry I was late. I had to stop for gas and the guy ahead of me kept putting the nozzle in and out and punching buttons on the pump and cursing when nothing happened." He chuckled. "Never seen a car refuse gas before."

Mom laughed. "You silly man." She set two pizzas in front of me. A bouquet of multicolored balloons jiggled on top of each box. "Happy birthday, sweetheart."

The aroma said "eat." My stomach said "no." I forced down a slice with Hawaiian toppings. The cheese under the pineapple burnt my tongue. I should have let it cool. *Stupid.*

No one else had any trouble. Maura-Lee sat prim and perfect, and ate and smiled and answered questions about school and Prince with short sentences that offered nothing extra. She never once looked my way.

"A bunch of hollow legs around here!" Mom said. "Bob, will you bring in another one?"

"But I worked so hard today," said Dad.

"So did I," Mom retorted.

"And I had an early lunch."

"So did I!"

Dad raised his voice. "But I can't run this machine without enough fuel!"

Maura-Lee put down her knife and fork and tucked her hands under the table.

Mom's eyebrows lifted. "Why don't you say what you mean? Why are you always so ... so ... *obtuse?*"

"Why are you always so ... so ... using such big words?" Dad pouted. He got up and carried the empties into the kitchen. Something hit the floor with a thud. "Oww! My leg fell off!" he bellowed. "It wouldn't have fallen off if I had time to digest my supper!"

"That was the hollow one," Mom shouted back. "And it wouldn't have fallen off if it wasn't full of coffee break pineapple upside-down cake. Frankie, run and get the duct tape so your father can tape his leg back on."

"Nah, it's okay," Dad called. "I did it myself."

He ferried in a third pizza, holding it high on one hand, waiter style. "Another for you, mademoiselle?" He swept a slice of The Works onto Bernie's plate.

"And you?" he asked Maura-Lee. She nodded.

"And Monsieur François?" I shook my head. He said sadly. "Le birthday boy needs more calories, n'est-ce pas?"

"The birthday boy's mother could use some more," said Mom, still chuckling.

"Oui, madame."

Mom stood and gave Dad a big kiss.

Dad returned it with energy. "What was that for?"

"For making me laugh."

"Is that a good thing?"

"And for being such a good kisser."

"Well, you're a good kissee!" Dad grinned happily. Mom hugged him tightly. "Oh, a Scronker!" Dad lifted her right off her feet.

"Enough already," said Bernie.

Dad put Mom down. "More fuel. Need more fuel."

Maura-Lee stared at my parents with a strange look on her face. I should have been mortified by their foolishness, but I was too full of miserable to have room for mortified.

When only one piece of the third pizza remained, Bernie asked me, "Time for cake?" I nodded. The sooner the cake, the sooner Maura-Lee went home, and the sooner I was left to my hell.

"Whose turn was it to decorate the cake?" Dad asked.

"Mine," said Bernie, "and it's perfect!" She disappeared into the kitchen for several minutes.

"What's taking so long?" Dad whined.

"Okay. Start singing now," Bernie ordered.

Mom started in too high a key. Dad struggled loudly. Bernie belted out way too many sharps and flats. Maura-Lee carried them all with a pure, clear voice. My family finished with a cheer and Mom laughed. "That's hard to sing!"

"And even harder to listen to!" said Dad, which got him a whack on the shoulder.

"Maura-Lee, you sing beautifully," said Mom.

"Ta-da!" Bernie said as the cake descended to table center.

Total silence.

It looked like someone had stomped on it. A

chocolate-frosted disaster straddled the width of the platter, its center flattened by a size-thirteen footprint, complete with tread marks and gravel ... no, not gravel — black gumdrops and butterscotch chips.

"It's a masterpiece!" Dad said softly.

"It's BRILLIANT! Quick, Bob, get the camera," Mom squealed. Then she noticed the look of horror on Maura-Lee's face. "It's the Ugly Cake Contest," she explained. "Anyone can make a *pretty* cake. We see who can make the *ugliest*."

"This," said Dad, his camera flashing, "this takes real talent. Smile, Frankie." Flash. "Now hold up your foot like you just stomped on the thing. Higher. Look maniacal. No. Scare me, don't depress me." Flash, flash.

"Frankie started the ugly cake thing," said Bernie.

"Yes, poor dear," said Mom. "He freaked out about the candles on his birthday cake. How old were you?"

Bernie answered for me. "Five."

"Frankie ran out into the rain and wouldn't come back in and we had to serve the cake under umbrellas. It got soaked and all the icing ran off. We made a game of it so Frankie would feel better. For years candles scared him, so we got out of the habit of using them. Instead we have the Ugly Cake Contest. We've eaten some genuine works of art!"

Dad started singing some strange song about a cake left out in the rain.

Mom joined in. There was no stopping them. All that could be done was to put fingers in ears and pray they didn't go for more verses.

Maura-Lee bit her lower lip tight in her teeth, as if struggling to hold something in. Her eyes said she was losing the battle. As Mom and Dad melded into a chorus of flat notes and laughter, Maura-Lee exploded out of her chair and tore out the back door.

CHAPTER 24

Release

"My singing isn't that bad!" said Dad.

"You two are totally embarrassing!" Bernie exclaimed.

"Don't be silly," said Mom. "Frankie, do you know what's wrong?"

"She's weird."

"Not as weird as Mom and Dad," Bernie smirked.

"Frankie," said Mom, "go make sure she's okay."

"Why me?"

"Because she's *your* guest."

"*You* invited her!"

"Go now!"

"We'll save you some cake," said Bernie.

There was no sign of Maura-Lee. I cut through the back-yard to College Street, figuring I'd head her off at the bridge. Part of me considered pretending I couldn't find her, but guilt kicked me forward. What was I going to say? I calculated my chances of surviving this encounter without a black eye at one in ten thousand.

She was already at the bridge. Just standing there, facing the river, gripping the thick aluminum pipe railing. I stopped out of fist range, hunted for the right words. I could say "I'm sorry, my parents are crazy," or just "I'm sorry." That always worked for Dad.

Instead I said, "I ... I didn't know anyone could move that fast in high heels."

She looked at me. Tears streaked her face. "I'm *sorry!*"

"Ah, um, no, *I'm* sorry. My parents can embarrass the spots off a leopard."

"No. It's *my* fault!"

"They go on like that all the time."

"It's *all* my fault!" she sobbed, choking out her words. "Your parents are so nice. I wanted *my* parents to be like that. I wanted them to *love* each other. That's why I did it."

"Did what?"

She shoved up her sleeves. Her tangled scars shone white in the evening light. I didn't know tears were contagious. I swallowed hard and fought to keep them behind my eyeballs.

Maura-Lee wilted against the railing. "They were out back fighting again, and the man and woman on TV had a beautiful candlelit dinner and they kissed and looked so happy and I thought if I put candles on the table ...

Mommy and Daddy would come in and finish eating ... and stop screaming at each other. I lit a candle, but it fell over. And the tablecloth ... I didn't know what to do."

The sadness in her voice hurt. "It was my fault," she whispered. "Children shouldn't play with matches."

"Hang on. Adults shouldn't leave matches where children can reach them! You were five years old! It *wasn't* your fault! Anyway, there wouldn't have been a fire if I had tried harder. I should have made *someone* listen."

"You were only five years old, too," said Maura-Lee. She sniffed and wiped the sleeve of her sky-blue sweater across her nose. "No one listens to five-year-olds." She locked her teeth over a quivering lower lip and took two deep breaths. "They were always fighting, always screaming in the backyard. As if I couldn't hear them out there. After my father and I got out of the hospital, she left."

"Sounds like she was going to leave anyway."

"She hates me ... everyone hates me."

"I don't."

"*Why?*"

I thought for a long moment. "Honestly? I guess because you're weird ... and if it wasn't for you, I'd have to be weird all by myself."

I swear she almost smiled. "You *are* weird, Uccello."

"Your father doesn't hate you, either."

"I know. But sometimes he makes me so angry."

"Yeah, parents."

Then she said quietly, "I get angry a lot."

"When Dad gets angry, Mom always asks him what he's afraid of. It seems to help."

Maura-Lee stood like a statue. The wind pulled a lock of hair from her galloping-horse hairclip and danced it across her face. After a minute she said, "I'm afraid a lot."

"Me too."

"You are not. You're the bravest person I know. You race around on that scary skateboard and act cool in front of Slug and you got on Prince when you were totally *orange!*"

I grinned. "So the trick is not to be orange?"

Maura-Lee sighed. "It's not easy."

The sun leaned on the horizon, pouring gold along the curve of river. A pair of black ducks swept past us, flying low, then flared their wings and tails into the wind and splashed onto the bright water.

"You want to come back for cake?" I asked.

Maura-Lee shook her head.

"Want me to walk you home?"

She shrugged. A soft blush crossed her cheeks.

We walked past the dairy and around the turn. The hillside cut the wind — a bit of calm, outside and in — and I felt like I could breathe for the first time all day.

Maura-Lee pulled her hair back into the clip. "I was wondering if you want someone with you when you let the petrel go. Dad could drive us to the ocean in the morning, before he takes me to Hug a Horse."

"I'd like that."

"Okay then. Same time, same place?"

"Yeah." I went as far as her driveway and watched her walk away.

"Did you find her?" Mom asked.

"Yup."

"So?"

"She wasn't feeling good all of a sudden. She said she was sorry."

"I see." I could tell she wanted more information, but didn't ask. She said, "Tim called again."

Tim! I'd forgotten Tim ... and Jelly Bean.

Mom said, "I told him you were out with a girl."

"You did *what?*"

"Well, you were."

"Mom! Now everyone on the planet will think I had a date with Maura-Lee!"

"Don't be silly. I didn't tell him who."

"Did he want me to call him back?" What would I say?

"Only if you can't get a drive."

"A drive?"

"To Hug a Horse."

"Huh?"

"Tomorrow morning." She frowned. "I assumed you knew. He said your birthday present is there. He made me promise to deliver you by nine — and he *knows* I like to sleep in on weekends." She pouted. "Is there any way you can go with someone else?"

"Yeah, no problem," I said. I could go with Maura-Lee — if I could ever face Tim again.

"Oh, goody. And speaking of presents ... BOB! BERNIE!" she shouted to the house. "Time for cake and presents."

"Did Tim say anything about Jelly Bean?"

"No."

Mom and Dad gave me a gift certificate for skateboard parts, Bernie had knitted me a really cool red toque, the latest style, and Maura-Lee's turquoise bag contained two skateboarding magazines and a photo mag with incredible shots of boarders in action.

I know the cake was delicious, but even a super dose of chocolate couldn't cure my dread of seeing Tim. What could I say? That I'm sorry I made Jelly Bean blind?

I stared at the TV for a while, then tried not to look the petrel in the eyes as I fed it. I failed and ended up crying myself to sleep, feeling more like four than fourteen.

My night got very crowded: I was trying to go skateboarding, but Tim and Kim, Maura-Lee and her father, Vanessa, Lana, Patsy, Michelle and Margaret, a whole herd of horses and even a flock of petrels stormed around me, flapping and shouting and shoving until I was nothing but a black streak on the pavement.

Morning brought me back to reality — the one with the habit of going from bad to worse.

I stood on the bridge as the hollow railing howled in the wind. I was getting sick of the wind. Under my arm, the petrel sat silently in its shoebox.

The Chisholms' pickup rattled to a stop and I climbed into the cab. We drove to the far end of the Antigonish Landing where the three rivers blended into the marsh. The sun sat a finger's width above the point, painting the world red-gold — of course, just like my dream. So this was the way it was going to be. Better get it over with. I was really glad I wasn't alone.

I opened the truck door. The air pushed in, thick and salty. The petrel scratched and bumped inside the box. It smelled home. So near ... I clenched my jaw and refused to cry.

We walked around the concrete vehicle barrier and along the dirt road with Wright's River rushing on our left and a large pond of tiny flashing fish on the right. Ducks floated among the reeds and seagulls dotted the open water. We stopped where a wide stretch of tall grasses touched the road.

This was the spot. Water flowed slowly between the red-gold hummocks. I set the box on the gravel and opened it slowly. The petrel sat up tall, craning its neck, eyes sparkling in the light. I lifted the creature one last time — felt the hard edge of wings, the teeny sharp claws, the trembling heart. I could barely breathe.

One last try.

Yes. One last try.

I raised my arms high, opened my palms and offered the petrel to the sky. The little bird didn't even stand. It spread its wings, leaned forward and fell.

Up.

Wings slightly bent — up and up and up — as soft as the light. With the tiniest twist of feathers it glided in a huge loop over our heads. Once around the compass. Then it turned into the wind, stroked its wings twice and sailed straight as an arrow toward the mouth of the harbor and the Atlantic Ocean.

Understanding slowly trickled into my brain. "The wind," I whispered.

"The what?" Mr. Chisholm asked.

I punched my fists at the sky and shouted, "THE WIND! THE WIND!"

"Of course!" Maura-Lee squealed. "It needed the wind to fly!" And she threw her arms around me and gave me a huge laughing hug. "It needed the wind to fly!"

I hugged her back. Her hair smelled like flowers.

Then she spun and leaped at her father, grabbing him around the shoulders and lifting her feet off the ground.

As she released him, he gasped, "What was that?"

"A Scronker," she laughed. "A real Scronker!"

A tear leaked down the good side of his face and he smiled — only a half-smile, but that was fine. Between Maura-Lee and me, there was enough smiling for a hundred people.

"Thank you," I said to him.

"Yes, thanks, Daddy," said Maura-Lee.

"Don't thank me," he said, his voice gravelly. "Thank the wind."

Maura-Lee crowed, "It flew! It flew! It flew! It flew! It flew!" And hopped around in little circles as if her feet meant to fly away, too.

"Okay, okay, calm down," said her father firmly. But he chuckled, a deep-down happy sound.

We rumbled back to town. I couldn't stop smiling. I rolled down the window, stretched out my arm and pressed a firm handshake onto the wind. "Thank you," I said silently.

"Drop you at home, Frankie?" Maura-Lee's father asked.

"Nope. I have to go to Hug a Horse Farm."

CHAPTER 25

The Surprise

My cheeks relaxed as we turned onto Meadow Green road. The combination of bad suspension and potholes did my bruised back no favors and I couldn't get comfortable on the worn bench seat.

Maura-Lee leaned over and said softly, "You can change the future."

I can? I dreamed the petrel was gone, that I put it down and a fox got it. But I *didn't* put the bird down in the grass — I held it up.

You can change the future.

We rattled past the scene of yesterday's accident. Past the crumpled royal-blue mailbox and Kim's white house. Past the mowed fields, thick forests and Tim's place. A squirrel ran onto the road and froze in the middle of our lane — its red-gold tail a quivering question mark. Keep going? Turn back? Keep going? Turn back?

The truck decelerated. "Make up your mind, squirrel," Maura-Lee's father ordered. We were nearly on top of the creature when it finally streaked into the ditch to live another day.

At Hug a Horse Farm, Jelly Bean wandered around the outdoor ring, sniffing out clumps of hay that the wind hadn't blown away. The morning sun glowed off her speckled white coat.

But she's blind.

Prince was in the pasture on the far side of the ring, nibbling at a drift of hay caught in the fence. When Maura-Lee shouted, "Hi, Prince," he raised his head and whinnied brightly.

"He likes you," her father said.

"He likes the carrots in my pocket. Do you want to come and see him?"

"Okay."

"Good morning, everyone," Vanessa said.

"The petrel flew away!" said Maura-Lee. "All it needed was the wind!" Then she looked at me. "Oh, sorry. That was Frankie's news."

I just smiled and shrugged.

"That's really wonderful," said Vanessa. "You should be very proud of yourself, Frankie. Maura-Lee, are you riding today? Prince certainly could use the exercise. He's been glued to the outdoor ring since you left. I think the old boy's fallen in love."

"That spotted pony's very pretty," Maura-Lee's father said. "Prince has good taste."

"That's Jelly Bean," said Maura-Lee, "the one I was telling you about."

"Tim and Kim are coming up early to see how she's doing," Vanessa told him. "They should be here any time now."

"I better be going, then," Mr. Chisholm replied.

Maura-Lee put a hand on his arm. "You could stay."

Her father looked at her like he wasn't sure he heard her right, but didn't ask her to say it again. "I'd like that," he replied.

"Good," said Maura-Lee matter-of-factly. "You can help me get Prince's tack on." She took his hand in both of hers and steered him into the barn. Then she reappeared in the pasture, dropped some carrots on the ground, shoved a halter up over the pillow of hair between Prince's short ears and led him inside.

I hung off the top rail of the fence trying to stretch a major cramp out of my lower back. The wind swooshed through the pine trees, like crashing waves.

Vanessa rolled a wheelbarrow into the ring and started scooping manure. She chatted constantly to the pony. "I'm over here, girl. Just me, picking up poo, picking up poo, that's what I do, picking up poo." She had about four forkfuls collected when a gust dumped the wheelbarrow. Jelly Bean leaped sideways and snorted, a sharp blast of air. Vanessa crooned, "Easy, girl. Easy."

"What happened?" Tim asked from behind me, his approach hidden by the wind. I jumped and my back jabbed.

"Just a little spook," said Vanessa. "She's fine."

No, she's not. She's blind.

Kim was with Tim. She leaned against the fence next to me. Her eyes were red and puffy. My chest tightened. "I'm *really, really* sorry about Jelly Bean," I said.

"It's not your fault," said Tim.

"Yeah, it is."

He frowned at me. "No. It's *not.*"

"*Yes, it is.* I saw the hoof prints on the road, and when Slug roared by I got Mr. Chisholm to speed up. It's my fault the truck was where it was when it backfired and made Jelly Bean jump on the car. If I hadn't said anything, the accident would never have happened. It's *my* fault."

Tim scratched his dense curls and nodded. "You know, you could be right. It *is* your fault," he said slowly. "So I have to thank you."

"*Thank me?* But ... but Jelly Bean is blind!"

"Yes, Jelly Bean is blind. And *was* blind. *Past tense. Before* she hit the car. She ran into the car because she *never saw it coming.* And if it hadn't been for the accident — if it hadn't been for you — we would never have gotten the vet out and discovered it in time to save what's left of her sight."

"What's left?"

"Yup. Dr. Jane said J.B. has only twenty percent vision in her left eye. But she still has fifty percent in her right eye. *Now* we have a chance to treat her ... thanks to you."

An earthquake of relief nearly shook me off my feet. "So you're not upset?"

"Of course I'm upset. My pony has equine recurrent uveitis! But *you're* not to blame, so get over that dumb idea."

Kim sighed. "I should have noticed something was wrong."

"She's used to you and your place," said Tim, "so she moves around like a normal horse."

"Except when she steps on my foot. And runs over cars!"

"But I saw her almost every day, too."

"And I saw her every week," said Vanessa. "This condition has likely been coming on for a few years. It explains why we thought J.B. was always picking fights with the other horses. She'd get inside their personal space and miss the body language that said 'back off,' so when she got kicked or bitten, she'd fight back."

"That's why she got snippy around people, too," said Tim. "When someone tried to pat her, it scared her. And I blamed it all on her personality."

"Poor Jelly Bean," said Kim, stepping through the wooden rails. Two apples plopped from her pocket. The speckled pony marched over and gobbled them up.

Vanessa laughed lightly. "Nothing wrong with her ears and nose!"

Kim hugged the pony's lowered neck. "So much for horse shows next summer."

"Oh, Kim," said Vanessa, "the shows would be tricky with so many horses in the ring. But how about dressage? One rider at a time."

"Perfect!" said Tim. "I was hoping to take The Ghost to a few dressage shows next year ... if it was all right with you, Kim. Now we could go together."

"So I can keep riding her?"

"Absolutely," said Vanessa. "Just stay off the road! And only ride in full daylight. Remember, *you* are her eyes, so you must always be a *rider*, never a *passenger*."

Kim smiled.

Tim gave me a poke in the shoulder. "Sorry I missed your birthday party, Frankie. What did the cake look like this year?"

"Dad got pictures," I said. "And Mom saved you a piece."

He almost drooled. "Got it with you?"

"No."

"Why not?"

"I didn't come straight here. I had to take the petrel back to the ocean first."

"Oh, sorry."

"No. It flew! Like, flew away!"

"You're kidding?"

"Nope. I just held it up and the wind took it. Simple as that. It flew right out to sea. Just sailed on the wind." I shrugged and grinned. "Who knew?"

Tim slapped me on the back. "You did it! You saved one, man! Way to go!"

The Freestar rolled in. Lana and Michelle and Margaret almost fell out, they were laughing so hard.

"That's the worst joke I've ever heard!" Michelle said.

"So why are you laughing?" Lana replied.

"I have no idea."

"What are you girls doing here so early?" Vanessa asked.

They exchanged sideways glances. "We came to see Jelly Bean," said Lana, clearly lying through her perfect teeth. "So, how is she today?"

"Same as yesterday," Tim said.

"Did she let you put the drops in her eyes?" Michelle asked.

Tim looked straight at Margaret. "Why are you *really* here?"

Margaret smiled, all freckles and innocence. "We came to watch."

"We're kind of early," said Lana. "But Mom has to go to Halifax for a Pony Club meeting."

"How are you getting home?" Vanessa asked.

"Oh, we're here for the day." She jiggled the bulging knapsack on her shoulders. "We've got sandwiches and juice and granola bars and potato chips and three kinds of cookies and —"

Michelle unzipped a bottom pocket. "And sunscreen and hats ... and nail polish and a toothbrush and a change of underwear —"

Lana screeched, "I do not!"

Michelle laughed. "You've got your whole bedroom in there!"

Lana loomed over her.

"Okay, maybe not the underwear."

"Come to watch what?" I asked.

"You," said Margaret.

Tim threw his hands in the air. "Thanks for ruining my surprise!"

"You haven't told him?" Lana giggled. "Then why's he here?"

The giggling was getting on my nerves. "I came for my birthday present," I said. I looked at Tim. "So, where is it?"

Vanessa's green eyes sparkled. "It's in the woods."

"Nuh-uh," said Lana, pointing. "It's in the pasture."

The only thing in the pasture was the herd of horses trotting toward us, The Ghost in the lead, black and shiny, long mane and tail flying in the wind. I peered at Tim. "What's going on?"

"Well, it's —" He flashed that fluorescent smile of his. "— the perfect birthday present. Now that you're into horses, I'm going to give you a riding lesson!"

"A *what?* Have you fried your CPU? I am not *into* horses. Never have been. Never will be."

Tim's smile melted. "Oh ... I thought ... the last time you were on Prince you were laughing and having so much fun. I really thought you'd get a kick out of a real riding lesson ... on The Ghost."

"The Ghost? If you think I'd *ever* get on *that* monster —"

Tim lit up. "Then how about Prince? We'll keep him on the lunge line. It'll be totally safe!"

Maybe it was because Tim was my best friend and he was upset about Jelly Bean and I had caused the accident (even if in a weird way it turned out to be a good thing). Or maybe it was because the petrel flew and I had this feeling deep-down inside that I'd never had before. Or maybe it was just because there were four pretty girls staring at me. Whatever the reason, I gave in. "Okay. A *short* lesson. Real short. But don't you think you should ask Maura-Lee first? It's her horse."

"Of course!" Tim exclaimed. He looked at the silver pickup. "Is that her dad's truck? Hey, we finally get to meet the guy?"

They all headed for the barn just as Maura-Lee and Prince stepped out the door, followed by her father. Everyone stopped like they'd hit a wall — except Kim. She moved in as smooth as a new skateboard on polished concrete.

"Hi, Mr. Chisholm," Kim said. "You're lucky, Maura-Lee. *My* father would rather hang from his toenails than go near a barn!"

Lana tried not to stare. Michelle elbowed Margaret to close her mouth. Then Tim marched over and put out his hand. "Hi, I'm Tim. Nice to finally meet you, Mr. Chisholm." Slick as a campaigning politician.

Maura-Lee's father put his gloved hand in Tim's and gave it a firm shake. His good eye shifted from face to face. Maura-Lee stood statue still. The wind rushed through the barn, lifting a cloud of fine dust above us. Prince leaned past Maura-Lee and whinnied loudly at Jelly Bean.

Tim grinned. "I think he has the hots for J.B. Are you going to ride him now?"

"She's going to show me what a good rider she is," Maura-Lee's father said.

Maura-Lee blushed.

"Great. So, Maura-Lee, what do you think about letting Frankie on Prince? I planned to give him a lesson on The Ghost — for his birthday — but he said he won't ride any horse but Prince."

"I didn't say that!"

Tim ignored me. "So what do you think? There's no hurry. Whenever you're done."

Maura-Lee squinted at me for several seconds. "No more orange, Uccello?"

I shook my head.

Tim raised an eyebrow at me. "Inside joke?"

"Oh, no," I replied. "No joke."

CHAPTER 26

The Gift

Maura-Lee led Prince and her father into the indoor arena.

Vanessa passed an apple-picker to Tim. "Lana. Michelle. There are two more in the barn. You know the drill. Pick-a-poo in the high traffic areas, under the lean-to, around the water trough, on the gravel feeding pads. Margaret, Strawberry found some burdocks. Her tail's a mess. Can you take care of that?

"You bet," said Margaret.

"Good. I've got saddles to clean. See you guys later."

Margaret fetched a hot-pink halter from the tack room and the reddish-brown pony from the field.

"I'll get the wheelbarrow," Tim said, and passed me his apple-picker.

I was surprised to discover that horse manure barely smelled once it had been out of the horse for a few hours. A strong wind didn't hurt, though. Picking poop wasn't as easy as it looked. It took practice to scoop things that rolled. Eventually Tim noticed my less-than-expert efforts and traded me the fork for the wheelbarrow. I had to take it to the manure pile every few minutes, which meant going through the top of the pasture. The herd had wandered into the woods, but I still kept a sharp lookout for them.

When we finished, Maura-Lee had Prince back in the barn. Her father stroked the horse's thick neck and talked softly to him. Maura-Lee was smiling like nobody's business.

"Your turn," she said.

Prince looked cute with his short teddy-bear ears and crinkly eyes.

Hang on. When did a horse become cute?

Good question. Was I losing my marbles or was Prince actually starting to look friendly?

Maura-Lee chuckled. "Careful," she said. "You're going pink."

"Yeah, right. Let's get this over with before I change my mind and Tim never speaks to me again."

I'll give my audience credit for being quiet, but having no audience would have been better. I put my foot in the stirrup and managed to climb aboard without trembling in my boots. Actually they were Tim's boots. Sneakers weren't allowed for "real" riding.

"Sit up straight," Tim ordered, "... not that straight. Relax a little ... now you look like a sack of potatoes."

"Make up your mind," I grouched.

"You have to hold your body in the right place but still give to the horse's movement. Like skateboarding. Too loose, you fall down. Too stiff, you fall down."

I shifted my position.

"Better. Now imagine if I yanked the horse out from under you. How would you land on the ground?"

"Ready to kill you."

"No, what part of you would hit the ground first?"

"My butt, of course."

"Right. You're sitting with your feet out in front of you, like you're in a chair. Sit on your seat bones, not your tailbone, and put some weight on your thighs and feet. The stirrups aren't just for getting up and down. Put some weight in them, like your legs are twice as long and you're standing on the sand."

I reached down with my feet.

"That's it! Feel better?"

"No."

Maura-Lee joined the girls on the bleachers. Tim stepped back, the long line in one hand, whip in the other.

"You're not going to hold his head?" I asked.

"I am," Tim said, "but from back here. Now give him a little nudge with your legs."

Prince walked. I was alone. Me and the horse. The eight other people didn't count. No one was at the horse's head, no one to stop him from leaping into the air and throwing me to the ground and ... I took a deep breath. So did Prince. Funny. We walked around and around, Prince stopping and starting when I did what Tim told me to do. That was actually kind of cool. Tim got farther away and I didn't freak out. Not bad. Not bad at all. Tim kept saying things about my legs and my back and my head and why it mattered, but most of it made no sense. "I hope you never plan to make a living teaching riding," I complained.

That's when the wind shifted. With a sudden freight-train roar it barreled through the big arena doors, launching dirt and hay and a fat white bucket straight at Prince. The bucket crashed into the horse's front legs. He leaped sideways, tripped, staggered two steps, went down to his knees with an enormous grunt, then heaved back upright. All in less than two seconds — two seconds that I stood in the stirrups and rode that giant fuzzy skateboard through the biggest ollie of my life.

"Look out!" Vanessa shouted. "The bucket is stuck on his leg!"

Prince was trembling, a coiled spring ready to pop. Tim was calling, "*Whoa, whoa-o-o,*" and running to shorten up the line, hand over hand. He grabbed Prince's bridle. Maura-Lee rushed over and ordered, "Foot, Prince. Give me your foot." Prince obeyed. The bucket hit the ground with a hollow clunk.

The beast totally softened under me. He stretched his neck out and blew a huge, nostril-flapping *blat* right in Tim's face. "Good boy," Maura-Lee said. Was she laughing? She was laughing! I nearly got killed and she was laughing! And the rest of them, too — whooping and applauding.

"Lord lifting lighthouses!" Tim cheered. "That was freaking amazing! *You* were freaking amazing. Man-oh-man-oh-man. I was sure we'd be digging dirt out of your ears. I know *good* riders who couldn't sit that. How did you do it?"

I shrugged. The adrenaline was wearing off. I felt all squishy inside. "Big skateboard," I replied. "Can I get off now?"

"After such a display of natural talent? Are you nuts?"

I didn't argue. My legs probably wouldn't have held me up if I had got off. So the lesson continued. Tim tried to get me to make Prince trot, but it wasn't happening. And things got a little weird when I found myself talking to Prince and smiling a lot.

When I was finally allowed to dismount, everyone clapped. Maura-Lee, grinning from ear to ear, led Prince away; but before she left she touched my arm, and said, "You did good, Frankie."

The girls invited Maura-Lee to stay for the day — they had lots of food in that backpack. Her father looked so happy, she agreed. Then he drove me home. On the way, he talked a surprising amount, mostly about birds. He really liked birds. When he dropped me off, he said, "Thank you."

It took me a moment to understand what he meant. I didn't know what to say. "I didn't do anything," I said quietly, but the wind pushed my words away. He smiled his half-smile and drove off.

That night I dreamed I flew. I'd had tons of flying dreams before, but this one was different. This time I knew age was gravity and this would be my last one. I was going to make the best of it. So I opened my wings, my red, red wings, leaned forward and let the wind take me away.